POON

POONA COMPANY

FARRUKH DHONDY

HARPER**PERENNIAL** MODERN**CLASSICS**

NEW YORK • LONDON • TORONTO • SYDNEY • NEW DELHI • AUCKLAND

HARPER PERENNIAL

Published in 2008 by Harper Perennial,
an imprint of HarperCollins *Publishers* India
a joint venture with
The India Today Group

© Farrukh Dhondy 2008

First published by Gollancz in 1980

ISBN: 978-81-7223-791-2

2 4 6 8 10 9 7 5 3 1

Farrukh Dhondy asserts the moral right to be identified
as the author of this book.

HarperCollins *Publishers*
A-53, Sector 57, NOIDA, Uttar Pradesh - 201301, India
77-85 Fulham Palace Road, London W6 8JB, United Kingdom
Hazelton Lanes, 55 Avenue Road, Suite 2900, Toronto, Ontario M5R 3L2
and 1995 Markham Road, Scarborough, Ontario M1B 5M8, Canada
25 Ryde Road, Pymble, Sydney, NSW 2073, Australia
31 View Road, Glenfield, Auckland 10, New Zealand
10 East 53rd Street, New York NY 10022, USA

Typeset in Perpetua Std 12.5/14
Jojy Philip New Delhi - 15

Printed and bound at
Thomson Press (India) Ltd.

To the memory of
Anil Madan

Contents

I

Cotton Figures

In the daytime a policeman in khaki shorts stood in the centre of Sarbatwalla Chowk, directing the flow of bicycles to and from the city, dodging the public buses which drove down the middle of the road and scattered traffic before them, shouting abuse at the drivers of the three-wheeled motorcycle rickshaws which swerved and lurched through the streets of our town like a tribe of drunken apes.

His constant argument with them was: 'You can't turn left, didn't you see my arm, you dolt, you bum? Show me your licence.'

The rickshaws insisted that they were allowed to turn left, to filter past his arm from Sachapir Street to Dastur Meher Road, the two thoroughfares that intersected at the Chowk.

'It's a British law,' the regulars who hung around the pavements outside the two cafes that graced the Chowk would say. 'This police fellow is too young to remember those days. If he'd tried to stop a sahib's carriage turning left, or even going straight, he would have felt their whip on his cheek. Too much power these fellows have.'

In fact the policeman had very little power. In the evenings after dark he'd don a white jacket and operate the red and green lights that hung above the crossroads on wires. When the regulars were feeling generous, if it had been a particularly good night for the gambling rackets they ran, they would send him a 'single char', a half cup of scalding tea from the Kayani or the Sachapir Cafe.

He was just a traffic cop and useful as a butt of abuse on the bad days when the police were unpopular for having conducted a raid on Uncle Frankie's or one of the other illegal booze distilleries in the alleys behind the Chowk. He didn't even share in the hafta or weekly bribes that the regulars and betting kings and bookies and hooch-sellers handed out to the senior members of the vice squad to keep them off their backs.

The Chowk was the heart of our neighbourhood, two hundred yards down Sachapir Street from where I lived. Our side of the Chowk was the city side and the other, towards Main Street, was the Cantonment side. The popular name for the Cantonment was the 'camp', so called because it was built by the British Raj for the soldiers and the administrators, growing out of the old city like a green branch on a wizened trunk. Sarbatwalla Chowk and our neighbourhood, a little way down the road, were distinctly in the bazaar part of the camp, where no soldiers or administrators would ever have lived but where they would have been allowed to wander to the shops and cafes and markets and tumble-down growth of a no-man's land between the narrow streets of the city and the spacious squares of the camp with its barracks and bungalows.

Even the rickshawallahs recognized Sachapir Street and the Chowk as the last outpost of the Cantonment. When they dropped my aunts or my grandfather outside our door, they would frequently argue about the extra money they wanted to charge for crossing the city limits from their normal beat. The Chowk was certainly the last stronghold of the hustlers of the camp, the touts and bookies who never expected clientele from the city, but were jealous of the business they cornered from Laxmi Road to East Street.

It was the hangout of everybody who was able-bodied and male in the neighbourhood. The rich stopped their cars there to pick up snacks, drugs, sweetmeats, flowers, to visit the dentist or one of the doctors who kept dispensaries around the Chowk. The poor hung about there because there was nothing better to do.

The two cafes were the hangouts of the older schoolboys, the college boys, the idle petty businessmen who ran the bakeries or the bicycle hire shops, the pious retired gentlemen with Parsi caps and newspapers who'd while away their hours in the bustle of company, the unemployed, the thieves, the layabouts and the few masters of the Chowk who lived, in one way or another, off them all.

Till I was twelve years old I hadn't been initiated into the ways and fare of the Chowk. It was a mystery and a place which put me on my guard about my self-confidence, my bearing, my ability to be a man among men who seemed to me constantly to chatter, fight, cuss each other, boast, argue about everything under the hot sun, swagger, sometimes even weep and most of all let their business and their personalities be known by all.

On the Chowk they called me nalha, small one, a word applied to anyone whose name wasn't important enough to be remembered. I only went to the Chowk and to the Kayani and Sachapir cafes when guests came to the house and my aunts or my grandfather took me out on to the back verandah, gave me some carefully counted change and asked me to go out by the back door, without letting the guests see the bottles I'd carry, to the corner cafe for a few almond lemons, sodas, raspberries, Vimtos or whatever.

Then regularly on the way to school, walking or, in later years, on bicycles, my friends and I would drop in to pick up a pack of chewing gum or a couple of sweets from the jars that stood on the glass counter, behind which the proprietors stood in shifts from six in the morning, till two the next.

One regular customer was Soli Kolmi, a baron of the Chowk. It wasn't his real name at all, but Kolmi, 'prawn', was what he was known as, because he was constantly bent double with a crooked back. He had a long nose and a vulturous neck, supple enough to allow him to hold his head up, and he wore a black felt cap on his thinning hair. He was scrawny and had deep hooded eyes like a bird.

His business was illegal gambling. He was the Chowk's chief bookie. When he wasn't sitting at a table in one of the cafes, he would squat on the concrete pavement, gathering scraps of paper which would be surreptitiously slipped to him with the names of horses and amounts of bets, or the numbers of the cotton figures game scribbled on them. In the mornings he collected slips. In the evenings he paid out. I had seen him do both, and knew, from early in my life, what he was up to.

It was not the kind of knowledge which I can say I acquired at a particular moment or over a definite period of time. My grandfather, though he had an occasional tea in the Chowk, never mixed with its citizens. He referred to them as loafers. I was forbidden to mix with them, but they were as much a part of the landscape as the tamarind and mango trees we were told not to climb. It wasn't a serious rule. We climbed the mango trees and mixed with the people of the Chowk as the part of boyhood we were proud of but didn't draw an adult's attention to unnecessarily.

The numbers' game, 'cotton figures' or 'satto-pancho' (seven-O-five) as it was called, was an ingenious invention.

As a child I was aware of intense discussion about numbers and probabilities. The game was played throughout the town and in Bombay, a hundred miles away, the capital city of our imaginations. It was a fairly simple game and was reputed to have made and marred many fortunes. What one had to do was, before seven o'clock each weekday evening, guess the numbers after the decimal point in the cost of a bale of cotton on the New York cotton share market.

As I said, I can't remember when the game was first explained to me, but I was aware that it was somehow one of the indications of a shrinking world. It was also evidence that America was a serious place, with share bazaars and prices and not simply a marvellous place where cowboys shot Indians and got slaughtered for their pains.

The hangers-on of the street corners in Poona were obsessively interested in the New York cotton market. It was legal to be interested in the figures but illegal to bet on them. The New York cotton market was like God. It was there, and always would be. Nothing that took place in our world could affect its workings. In one day the opening price would be 37.85 and the closing price 38.22. It was the '85' and the '22' that you betted on. If you backed one pair and the newspapers declared that evening that it had come up, you gathered winnings at nine to one. If you predicted both the opening and the closing pairs, you gathered odds of between eighty and a hundred to one.

In the end the bookies got rich and like other businessmen claimed that the risk justified it.

Kolmi took betting slips from anyone – from the rich, the poor, the unemployed, the intelligent, the ditherers, the beggars and policemen, but not from the young.

If I or my friends wanted to place a bet, we had to do it in the name of someone else. I never betted, I never had the money and felt that betting was wicked. My friend Kishan betted and Dinsy, who was still in school and was born into a family of punters, betted boastfully. Dinsy was probably the only schoolboy from whom Kolmi accepted the four anna bet, probably because his dad had already been round and placed a couple of rupees.

The first time I ever placed a bet with Kolmi was on behalf of Eddie the Inventor. He lived in a one-room flat in alleys which led off Dastur Meher Road. The only thing that people in the Chowk knew about him was that he was called Eddie because he had been born on the day King Edward VII died and his parents had called him 'Edul', a good Parsi name to preserve their prestige, but had referred to him as Eddie ever since because they felt that somebody had to carry on the royal tradition. That seemed to be the only known fact about him. There were opinions and rumours about the old man. My grandfather always said that Eddie had come to Poona because his father had run some sort of pirate trade in the Indian ocean and he had arrived in town in rags and without an anna to his name years ago after the pirate craft had been shipwrecked and all his family killed. The rest of the neighbourhood said he was crazy.

Eddie had constructed his own bicycle out of spare parts. No one could say where or how he earned his living. There was once a rumour in town that he was a spy paid by a foreign power, but the people who spread that story couldn't say for whom he was spying, because at the time India wasn't at war with any nation in the world. Eddie would mooch around town on his bicycle, wearing a solar topee and a white jacket, with bicycle clips on his trousers. He told people that he was an inventor and a scientist.

I made friends with Eddie quite by coincidence. My school used to have sports in the evenings in the centre of the race-course which was one of the wide open spaces of the Cantonment. At a particular time of year, a crocodile of two hundred boys would be marched up to the racecourse and made to run around its perimeter inside the railings, to build stamina for the annual cross-country race. I would put my spectacles in the pocket of my white shorts because the sweat from the effort of running would cause them to slip on my nose. At that age my spectacles were my prized possession. I loathed them and relied upon them. One day at the end of the run, just as the dusk was gathering and the whole crew of runners had been lined up to be dismissed by the teacher in charge, I felt in my pocket and found my specs missing.

The parade of runners was dismissed. Khushroo said he'd help me look for them. We walked round the track we had already covered three times at a trot. It was getting dark. There was no sign of the spectacles and I was afraid of what my grandfather would say when I got home without them. Khushroo was sympathetic. He kept raking the coal track we'd been running on to see if they'd been trodden under.

The racecourse was deserted. We had searched for an hour without any success and I was steeling myself to go home and face the music when in the gathering dusk we saw a figure in front of us. It was Eddie, whom we knew by sight and reputation. He had his bicycle on the grass and was sitting cross-legged in the middle of the running track with a contraption spread in front of him.

'You haven't seen a pair of spectacles?' Khushroo asked him.

Eddie couldn't hear what Khushroo said because he had a pair of headphones strapped to his head and was fiddling with the dials of a complex instrument built into a large wooden box. By his side, in his left hand, he held the sort of metal horn that one used to see on old phonographs.

Watching Eddie, it struck me that the man was really crazy, listening to old phonograph records in the middle of the racecourse when it was nearly night. Khushroo went and tapped him on the shoulder and Eddie took the headset off, looking annoyed. Khushroo repeated his question.

'I say, listen to this,' Eddie said and as Khushroo leaned over him he put the headphones to his ear.

'What can you hear?'

'Some drumming,' Khushroo said.

'Horses. Horses' hooves. One mile away.'

'I say, good thing, yaar,' Khushroo said to me, forgetting about our search.

'Listen. Have a listen.'

'Yes,' I said, 'I can hear. What is it?'

'Big Ear,' Eddie said.

'Big Ear?'

He explained that the Big Ear was really an amplifier which could pick up sounds from a mile or two away.

'Only problem with it is, boys, it can't separate one sound from another. Only the human brain can do that.'

I had never heard anyone speak like that.

'What is it you two boys are looking for?' said Eddie.

8

'A pair of specs, Farrukh's specs.'

'Here they are,' Eddie said. 'I'm afraid they're broken.' He pulled the spectacles out of a cloth bag that lay next to him.

'I never pass anything over,' he said.

Eddie had picked them up from the track. One of the lenses was smashed and the plastic of the frame was badly twisted. I looked at them.

'Don't worry. I can make you a new lens,' Eddie said. 'Where do you boys live?'

We told him. I was relieved about my specs, wondered whether he could really get me a substitute lens for the broken one and very curious about the Big Ear and about Eddie.

Eddie packed up the Big Ear, wrapping its wires around the battery and strapping the big horn on to the handlebars of his bicycle. We followed him into the valley where he lived, thankful for the dark which had descended. Neither Khushroo nor I wanted to be associated openly with Eddie.

His door was padlocked from the outside. He opened it carefully and spent a few minutes bringing the equipment of the Ear in and packing it carefully into a crowded corner. It was the most incredible room we had ever seen, lit by a fluorescent lamp which wasn't fixed to the ceiling, but hung by a chain arrangement on pulleys. There was an old table under the light and on the table a jumble of old electronic equipment. It seemed as though there were headphones everywhere and copies of *Popular Mechanics* and *Popular Electronics* thrown all round the room. The room was full of evidence of tinkering, but no evidence of living. Through the back door I could see some shirts hanging on nails on the wall of a smaller room.

'This is the laboratory, boys,' Eddie said, sitting down on a three-legged wooden stool. 'Now give me those specs.'

From the corner of the room he fetched a cardboard box and a pair of calipers. There were hundreds of spectacle lenses in the box. He raked through them, pulled out a few and measured them between the calipers.

'It won't be exact,' Eddie said, 'but one of these three or four should be all right. Hold them to your left eye and look through them.'

I did as he said. He was right. One of the lenses was nearly right for me.

'Will it fit the frame?' I asked.

'Not till tomorrow,' he said, 'I'll have to grind it down.'

'How can I go home without my glasses? My grandfather will kill me.'

'I'll put in another one which is no good but fits the frame. You just stop looking through that eye. No one will know,' he said. He grinned and the lines on his cheeks became deep folds.

It was an acceptable solution. I had to go back the next day. He was true to his word. He did get the lens to fit the frame and saved me a scolding. That was how our friendship with Eddie began.

Khushroo and I went to his room several times after that and watched him tinkering with valves and wires and soldering irons.

He was building the most sophisticated system of radio communications outside America, he told us. He never let us tinker with his serious work, but he taught us, over the weeks, how to build crystal sets, how to lay out a circuit of wires on screws on a board of wood, how to tune a trimmer condenser and how to make neat soldering joints.

'The Big Ear is nothing. You wait till this boy starts his work.'

The 'boy' grew from day to day. Eddie had gathered old army surplus chassis, olive green metal cabinets with holes in them and had fished around for secondhand valves in the thieves' market that assembled under the Sangam Bridge on Sundays.

When the Big Boy started working, Eddie couldn't contain his excitement. He put the headphones over my ears and frantically fiddled with the knobs.

'What's coming through?'

'All sorts of bleeps and buzzing and the sound of the sea,' I said.

'It all means things, signals, nalha, signals. I'll be rich. This is it.'

The next day when I went back Eddie was secretive.

'I want you to do something for me before seven o'clock.' He dug in his pocket and pulled out a five rupee note. 'You know I'm not a gambling man, nalha. But don't misunderstand this. Take this money and go to the Chowk and put all the money with Soli Kolmi on "69". Write it on a betting slip and get a receipt.'

I clutched the money in my fist.

Eddie brought his face right down next to mine. I could smell his breath as he whispered through his brown teeth, 'Don't tell anyone who gave you the money or whose bet it is. They don't take cotton figure bets from me. Tell them it's your grandfather's.'

At the Kayani everyone was poring over the morning papers. There was an argument in progress. For the last week the papers had been full of the first Russian space adventure. The USSR had launched their satellite and 'Sputnik' and

'Gagarin' entered the talk at school, at home, in the streets, in the Chowk.

Dinsy was saying that he had actually seen Sputnik, like a star with neon light. The morning newspapers had quoted a scientist in Bombay who doubted the fact that the Russians had launched a space satellite. He had told the press that in his opinion the photographs that we had all seen were taken in a studio and the USSR had pulled off one of the biggest confidence tricks in history by releasing stories about the satellite months before it was launched.

'It's communist propaganda,' Kolmi was saying.

I went up to him.

'Mr Kolmi,' I said. I didn't want to hand him the betting slip or the money in front of anyone.

'Yes, little man?' he said, turning round.

'I have some business with you.'

'With me?'

He was as surprised that I had spoken to him as I was.

'Will you just come this side,' I said. We turned our backs on the argument and I uncoiled my fist with the money and the slip which said '69'. I knew that Kolmi didn't give receipts, I wouldn't even ask for one. He would laugh.

'What's this, what's this, what's this? You know the rules, little one. We don't take money from minors.'

'It's for my grandfather,' I said.

'Your grandfather?' Kolmi looked amazed.

It was an implausible lie. Everyone on the Chowk knew that my grandfather was an upright, upstanding citizen, more likely to send the police round to the bookies than to use their services.

'Is he sick?' Kolmi asked.

'He said to take the bet, but not to make it public.'

'Whew,' Kolmi said. 'The priests and Jesuits I can understand. They like a little game now and then, but your grandfather? Are you sure he gave you this?'

'Where would I get five rupees?'

Kolmi pocketed the money. He seemed to understand it was a delicate situation.

'All right,' he said, 'all right, we'll see.'

'He also said that if he wins, you mustn't stop him in the Chowk when he comes back from his evening walk in Main Street. You must give me the money.'

He nodded solemnly, like a family doctor who understood about keeping secrets.

The number didn't win. When the results came in, the winning number was passed around the Chowk by word of mouth. I went back to Eddie and told him.

He didn't look discouraged. Instead he brought out some manuals and began leafing through their pages.

'First time unlucky. I'll crack the code, nalha. Those Russians can't fool me. I'll be rich, wait and see.'

I didn't know what he was talking about and didn't ask.

A few days later he asked me to place another bet for him and again swore me to secrecy. Again he lost.

The third time he won. He won magnificently. Kolmi drew me aside and asked me to step outside the Sachapir Restaurant with him into the shadows of the alley at the back. He counted out four hundred rupees. I had never seen so much money in my life. I stuffed it in the pockets of my shorts and went back to Eddie.

'You've won.'

'Hand it over,' Eddie said and he rattled the notes in his hand. 'Tomorrow again. I've cracked the code.'

Ten times Eddie sent me out in the evening to place bets on his behalf with Kolmi. It became a ritual for me. The amounts he put on the bets became increasingly large. Only once out of those ten times did he win. I would draw Kolmi aside and give him the money. He'd accept it, but it seemed to sadden him.

'Such a good man like your grandfather,' he would say. 'Tch, tch, tch,' and he'd shake his head wondering what the world was coming to, and pocket the money.

In the evenings my grandfather took his walk. Wearing a pair of woollen trousers and a long black Parsi jacket and flourishing a walking stick, he'd walk down to Main Street and sit with friends from his generation on chairs which the proprietor of Fisher's Hatshop, at the corner of Sachapir and Main Street, provided for the gang. They'd sit there all evening and talk about the old times; about stretcherbearing in the First World War in Abyssinia, about the foreclosures on mortgages on the houses of the bankrupt and unlucky, of news of bailiffs rushing in to sell the furniture of discredited debtors, of the corruption of the Indian police and the good old days of British rule when fewer loafers and touts were allowed to operate and alcohol was legal and the price of a bribe was much higher and bribetakers had finesse and subtlety, unlike the bold-faced dogs who had been made officials in the Indian Raj.

When he returned by way of the Chowk, my grandfather would look neither this way nor that, his evening's gossip and moan having put him even more against the riff-raff of the Chowk than when he set out pious and freshly shaven each evening.

It was on one of these walks back that Kolmi made bold to greet my grandfather. Kolmi was sitting on the pavement outside the Kayani with a few other stalwarts, taking the evening air and waiting for the boy who came screaming down the street each evening with the late night edition of the '*Bhonga*', the *Daily Trumpet,* which was published and bought for the sole purpose of making known to the town the cotton figure results from New York.

'Sahebji, Sahib,' Kolmi said to my granddad.

My grandfather was astounded at being addressed from the pavement.

'Oh yes, Sahebji,' he said, trying to hurry on.

'It's quite cold today, not like Poona,' Kolmi said, trying to strike up a conversation that would make his companions feel that he had traffic with people of the neighbourhood who considered themselves gentlemen.

'Yes,' my grandfather said and hurried on.

The others laughed and Kolmi stood up.

'What's the matter? Not good enough for you?'

My grandfather turned round contemptuously.

'You find it cold? Buy yourself a sweater from your ill-gotten money.'

'Oh I see, it's like that is it? Your grandson didn't lose twenty rupees with me yesterday. You weren't ashamed to take four hundred rupees the other day and six hundred rupees the next.' Kolmi dug in his pocket and brought out the betting slip I had given him earlier that evening. 'It's three and five this evening, isn't it Lord-sahib?'

'What is this you're rattling about? Who takes money from you?' my grandfather said. People came out of the restaurants at the sound of Kolmi's raised voice.

Dinsy caught me on the way from Eddie's, told me the story and described the scene.

'He called your grandfather a liar in front of fifty people.'

15

My heart sank into my canvas shoes. How could I go home now? Dinsy said he could see my problems. He said I was too young to have such worries and maybe a cup of tea would clear my head. I refused the invitation. I went back to Eddie's. He'd be waiting for me to fetch the results and the money he was certain he would win. What would I say to him? I walked down his alley and then before I reached his door I turned back. I had to go home. I had to face my grandfather. There was nothing else to do.

On the way home I met Dinsy again. I had tears in my eyes. I shouldn't have taken Eddie's bets to Kolmi. I wasn't that kind of boy. Yes, there were boys who were drawn into the ways of the Chowk and some of them were my school friends and people whose houses I was in and out of, but my grandfather didn't understand. He always talked about the British and how the 'sahibs' were good people and how the soldiers that had been sent over never had a bath, and about Nehru and Gandhi and their lot ruining our country. He didn't understand as even I did, that Kolmi and his kind took their chance where they found it. A quick rupee, a quick answer was their creed.

The lights of our verandah were on when I got back. Dinsy was trailing me.

'Don't be afraid, nalha, just tell the truth.'

What he would do to me I didn't know. My grandfather had never beaten me. My aunts, who would also be at home, had only hit me with the back of a brush when there wasn't time to do anything else about my disobedience. My mother and father were far away in another town. It struck me that I could ask Eddie for some money and go to the railway station and run away from home to my mother and father. But no, I couldn't do that. I had made a fool of my grandfather in the

Chowk. The whole neighbourhood would now think that he was a punter and there would be no dignity left to us.

'How was it done, mischief?' was the first thing my grandfather said. He came to the door as I opened the wooden gate and walked up the three stone steps of our verandah.

'I'm sorry,' I said.

Dinsy stood on the pavement outside our gate. My grandfather was in his pyjamas and over his shoulder I could see the anxious faces of my aunts. Behind them stood my sister, looking as scared as I felt.

'So you've decided to come home,' one of my aunts said.

'It's the usual time,' I said.

'You want to enter this house and sleep in your bed?' my grandfather said.

I didn't want to look into his eyes. I looked at the flag-stones that made up our verandah and started counting the cracks that had appeared in them. I hadn't noticed the cracks before. I was hoping that his anger would break like a wave over me. I wanted it over.

'So you've become a gambling man?' my grandfather said.

'No sir,' I said in Gujarati.

'You are ashamed of your short pants. You want a beard now? You want my white hair?'

'No sir.'

There were twenty-seven cracks in the flagstones. I had played on that verandah ever since I was three. Why hadn't I noticed them before?

'So Soli Kolmi is your friend and agent is he?'

'No sir.'

'Just give him one slap,' my aunt said.

'Don't let the neighbourhood hear our troubles,' my grandfather said. 'Come inside.'

17

He sent my aunts and my sister away from the front room. He sat in the easy chair and asked me to stand. The slap I expected, even wished for, didn't come. He was intrigued. He wanted to know where the money came from .

'Eddie.'

'When have you been going to see Eddie?'

'Just a few times, he shows us electronics.'

'He is a black-faced dog.'

The tears were rolling down my cheeks, but I wasn't crying, my breath was normal and the words were coming out of my mouth automatically.

I was telling my grandfather about Eddie's spectacular discoveries. Sputnik gave out signals. The Russians were relaying the New York cotton figures to the whole world. Eddie knew the secret code they were using. He had built himself a receiver with the frequency of the Sputnik transmitter. He could find out the results of the cotton figures game twelve hours before they were announced. He had taught Khushroo and me to make crystal sets. When the code became completely clear he would be rich. The bookies in Poona didn't know that the Russians were giving out the cotton figures every day. Yes, he did swear me to secrecy. Yes, it was he who told me to use my grandfather's name when I placed the bets.

'I have protected that scoundrel too long,' my grandfather said. 'Do you know who he is? He spread the story about being shipwrecked himself and none of us have said anything about it these forty years. He was thrown out of the Army Signals Corps for falling asleep when important messages were coming through in the war. He is a rascal.'

When my grandfather paused, I could hear the shuffle of feet and voices on the verandah. My grandfather rose from his chair and went to the door. There was a scurry of feet. Intruders. I rushed to the door and saw Dinsy and three other neighbours dash through the gate and disappear down Sachapir Street.

For a week I didn't go to the Chowk or to see Eddie. Then on my way back from school Dinsy stopped me in the Chowk and told me what had happened. They had overheard my explanation to my grandfather. One of the boys had told Kolmi and that night a delegation from the Chowk had visited Eddie's place. Kolmi was furious. He walked in shouting at Eddie and began to smash the place up.

'I'll teach you to spoil my business with satellites,' he shouted.

'Mistake,' Eddie shouted back. 'Mistake. Mr Kolmi, forgive me. I am a scientist. Don't do this to me, I am a poor man.'

Every piece of equipment in the room was smashed to bits: the Big Ear, the Big Boy, the crystal sets. Every magazine was shredded by Kolmi and the other bookies who had stormed the house.

I met Eddie three weeks later, bicycling up to the racecourse as the boys from school were returning after games. He called to me. He didn't look repentant or damaged.

'I am a scientist and an inventor,' he said. 'These little things don't stop me. You know why we didn't win every day and clean the bookies out? I'll tell you the truth, nalha, Big Boy wasn't powerful enough. I was catching Poona Military airport signals. But the next stop is Sputnik. If you come tomorrow I'll show you how to build a valve set now that you're getting older. Some damn good designs have come in *Popular Electronics*.'

II

Samson

There was only one creature who constantly haunted the crossroads and he was called Samson. He actually lived on the Chowk. Not above it, not two hundred yards away from it, not in the houses in the alleys behind it, but on the pavements outside the Kayani and Sachapir cafes. He had picked up his nickname because he had long, black hair down to his podgy shoulders. He must have had another, perfectly good Parsi name, but 'Samson' was what we knew him as.

He was massive. Fat hung about his face, wrinkled and dangling like the jowls of a bulldog. Counting his chins was a competition on the Chowk. People said he ate three chickens at a go and five platefuls of rice a day. His belly hung over the tight cord of the white pyjamas he wore day and night. His shirt looked like a bedspread. He walked in the fashion which was popular with the people we called 'heroes', his arms stretched into stiff bows on either side of his body, legs wide and feet pointed outward. It was supposed to tell people who were watching that your muscles were so thick they prevented movement.

Samson would sit with Kolmi on the pavement outside the Kayani restaurant, waiting for betting slips or for the results of the cotton figures racket to be declared. He would be in and out of the restaurants. He hardly ever left the Chowk.

He didn't bet, didn't smoke, didn't drink and never had a regular job. He earned some food by being the unofficial night watchman on the Chowk, paid by the owners of the Sachapir and the Kayani in cups of single char and platefuls of rice, which he'd eat when the cafes closed their doors and cleaned out their kitchens at two in the morning. The only work he ever got paid for was body-carrying. When a Parsi of our neighbourhood died, Samson would shroud himself in the white muslin coat and pyjamas of the khandias and help carry the corpse on a wooden bier through the town to the Towers of Silence on the hill beyond Golibar Maidan where the community left its dead to be eaten by vultures.

Funerals were, of course, occasional employment. The fees he got for leading the team of shoulderers would pay his debts to the betel-nut wallahs and buy him the meat that charity wouldn't afford.

Late at night if I passed through the Chowk, I would see Samson laying out the bundle of blankets which the owners of the Kayani allowed him to keep in the corner behind the counter. His bed was one of the cement parapets outside the cafes.

'Still awake, Samson?'

'Oh it's you, nalha. I'm just checking the locks on the Ahura Cycle Mart and Kaiko's Chemist's shop. Doctor Bharucha forgot to put the padlock on his dispensary today.'

There was the story of how he'd surprised two thieves breaking into the Ahura Cycle Mart one night. In his excitement he had mangled three bicycles instead of the thieves. There was also the story of how Samson had dealt with the Gurkha who had presented himself in a smart khaki uniform to the shopkeepers of the Chowk and had been appointed by them as the official night watchman. The Gurkha, with his five foot wooden stick and reputation for bravery, had challenged Samson's right to loiter and sleep in the Chowk and check the locks of the shops he had guarded for many a year.

'The pug-nose is looking for trouble,' Samson had said.

The Gurkha had been found by the sweepers of the gutters below the bridge at the end of Sachapir Street one morning, alive but with a broken back, staunchly refusing to tell the police how his stick came to be in three pieces and how he had accidentally fallen from the bridge into the gutter.

Samson was to me the symbol of the Chowk. No one could tell me the story of how he came to be there. Some said that he had lived with his mother in a house in the City after his father died and they had been thrown out by the landlord because his mother took to entertaining 'boyfriends'. Others said that he had been brought to the Chowk from Pakistan by kidnappers when he was a child and had never developed the sense to go back. Where he washed and bathed was a mystery.

As children we would gather round him and ask him to show us his muscles. He'd put his hand on his head and make his biceps dance. He'd run his fingers through his tresses and curls and say he got his body from God and his strength from not using it very often.

'Work weakens the spirit, spirits weaken the work,' he would say. Samson never said very much. The first time I heard him string together more than two sentences was when we were sitting at the Sachapir cafe, trying to feel, at the uncertain and miserable age of thirteen or fourteen, part of the crowd that hung around there.

Samson was the only regular of the Chowk who conde-scended to acknowledge our presence and to talk to us. He sauntered into the cafe and came towards where Ashish, Kishan, Shahid, Dara and I were sitting with our cups of single char. He sat at our table without a word, looking at the notice which said *Do Not Spit* and making us unsure whether he was deliberately gracing us with his company.

'Do you want a char?' Kishan asked.

Samson just held up his hand, refusing the offer.

Kolmi and some others drifted in and dragged the wooden chairs around the other tables to ours.

'Why is your face registering half-past six?' Kolmi said to Samson.

'Thinking,' Samson replied.

'He has to think to digest his food nowadays. No exercise.'

'The rich,' Samson said, still staring at the notice forbidding spitting. He turned his head and spat.

'What about them? Two eyes, two ears, hands, feet, just like you, only thinner,' Kolmi said.

'They don't die fast enough,' Samson said. He patted his belly with both his hands. 'No good funerals in the neigh-bourhood for six months.'

'It's these new-fangled, sister-fucking doctors. They cure people just by holding up their degrees from England and America,' Kolmi said. 'Kill one doctor and you'll have plenty funerals, plenty chicken to eat.'

'No job for weeks,' Samson said. 'The last time we carried old man Bhot to the tower, his relatives were all wearing canvas shoes like us. Stingy beggars from Bombay. I got eight men together. Two of these children could have carried the old man, he was so thin. We walked so fast the relatives at the funeral who were following the body couldn't keep up. They told the priest that we were all drunk.'

Samson shifted his weight with indignation. Everyone knew he didn't drink.

'I need a tarpaulin now that the monsoon is coming,' Samson said.

'Don't worry, somebody's bound to die. The heat is sure to kill a couple of oldies,' Kolmi said.

'I've heard some rumours. Rumours of sickness in high places,' Samson said. 'We vultures have to keep our eyes and ears open.'

He seemed to be talking to us now. I caught his eye. It moved from me to Kishan to Ashish.

'Do you know what vultures do, boys?' Samson asked.

No one said they did.

'I'll tell you what they have to do. They have to look around and see what's coming to them. You know what I get to eat? Do you hear the waiter shouting "One rice-plate with chicken curry"? I sit here in the evenings and wonder if there'll be any chicken curry left when the cafe closes. Stuff they can't keep in their damned refrigerator.'

'I'll buy you a bread and butter. Just ask decently,' Kolmi said.

We'd never seen Samson in this mood before. Normally he was jovial and never talked about himself or his livelihood.

'Thanks, I've eaten a bellyful of curses today,' he said to Kolmi. 'What have you eaten today, Ashish, big boss?'

Ashish was startled. He hadn't expected Samson to address him directly. Before that I wasn't even sure that he knew our names.

It was more probable that he knew Ashish's name because he came from one of the influential families of our neighbourhood. For three generations now, his family had owned the ice-factory next to the fire temple on Synagogue Street, and had grown rich enough to donate to its funds and interfere in its politics. The Kayani mob, Jamshed and his brothers and their father and uncles, owned the bakeries of the Cantonment and a few restaurants, but their riches were a generation deep. Ashish's family had ancestral weight and one of the biggest bungalows in the neighbourhood. They didn't like him hanging around the Chowk, didn't like the company he kept and didn't allow him to get matey with the labourers and block pushers who worked in the ice factory.

Ashish dressed like the rest of us but his clothes were always more expensive. His silk shirts and tapered trousers were washed by the laundry and smelled of Lux. He wore expensive Kolhapuri chappals and in his pockets he carried a pack of American cigarettes and a hundred rupee note which showed through the fine cottons and silks.

'If you did some work you could eat what you liked,' Ashish said.

This was not a good thing to say to Samson. A hush fell on the company. Kolmi's eyes rolled up to the heavens. It was his way of saying that he wanted no part of the argument that would follow. The rest of us, Ashish's crowd, distinctly felt a blunder had been made. Samson weighed two hundred and twenty pounds.

'How much ice did your family make today?' Samson asked. He was cool, pretending not to be particularly in-terested in the conversation and looking around at the other people in the cafe as though he was waiting for someone.

'There's a lot of sweat in making ice,' Ashish said. 'Our workers don't sit in the Chowk all day and wait for people to die.'

'This is a boy,' Samson said, turning to Kolmi, 'this is just a puppy of a boy, whose family work with water. He talks a lot of steam.'

'No need to get offensive,' Ashish said. 'If you can't get any work carrying dead bodies, come to me at the office and I'll see that my father gives you a good job.'

Samson's eyelids dropped. He seemed to be saying a prayer to himself. Then he cleared his throat and spat to the left of his chair. The proprietor of the cafe came out from behind the counter.

'Look don't do that kind of thing here,' he said to Samson. He pointed to the notice on the wall, brown with age, which said 'No gambling. No alcoholic beverages, no spitting'.

'I'll clean it up at night,' Samson said, 'after you close down.'

The proprietor shook his head and went behind his counter again.

'The trouble with most of the people in the Chowk,' Ashish said, 'is that they don't want to do any honest work.'

He was echoing his father. We had heard his father say the same thing when we gathered round him and were told for the hundredth time the story of how his father had been an immigrant from Iran and worked hard to save enough to buy ice blocks from the British owners and break them up in a special way and sell them at a discount to the small cafes who couldn't afford to buy a whole block at a time.

'Your grandfather was the biggest bootlegger in the Chowk,' Samson said. 'What do you know about it? Got rich first by turning his brothers to the bottle.'

'If you worked like my grandfather worked,' Ashish said, 'you wouldn't be so bloody fat.'

It was turning nasty. Kishan said he had to go home. Dara said his mother wanted him to pick up some medicine from the dispensary. Shoes began to shuffle under the table. This sort of argument would ruin our chances of sitting around the Sachapir cafe for weeks.

Kishan got to his feet and said an awkward good-night. Ashish's face was set stubbornly. He knew he'd crossed the big boys.

Kolmi looked up at the ceiling. His Adam's apple jumped up and down. 'Ashish,' he said, 'Samson has sons as old as you pushing rickshaws in Singapore. Don't tell him anything.'

But Ashish was bent on a fight. Kishan left and Dara left and I was left alone with Ashish and Kolmi and Samson. My mind raced for an excuse I could use to get away too.

Ashish was beginning to say that India was finished because the people didn't want to work. His brother had a degree in economics and he knew about these things. Kolmi and Samson were listening with impassive faces.

'If you make ice, that's something,' Ashish said. 'My brother told me. If you cut somebody's hair, then you're not making anything. My father wants to open a tractor factory, you know, out in Pimpri, and that will really help the country.'

'Is your father going to make all the tractors himself?' Kolmi asked.

'We have the know-how,' Ashish said, 'just like we know how to make ice.'

My excuse came to me. 'I'd better be getting home,' I said. 'I've got to teach my little sister her prayers before she goes to sleep.'

'Prayers?' Samson said. 'You'd better be getting home and saying some prayers for your grandmother, Ashish. I hear she's not in very good health.'

I was already on my feet. Everyone in the neighbourhood knew that Ashish's grandmother was dying of cancer. In the last week the doctors had been called three times and it was rumoured that Ashish's father didn't want her to go to hospital because if she was out of the house, from under the gaze and care of her daughters-in-law, she might change her will. She might leave all her money, including the ice factory, to charity or to the fire temple. That was the gossip.

I got to my feet.

'Well you'd better be going too, Mr Ashish,' Samson said.

'Yes, I have to go,' Ashish said.

'Pay for the tea as you go out,' Kolmi said.

Six days later Ashish's grandmother died. We had to go to the funeral. We wore our white laced muslin tunics, white trousers and black pointed-toe shoes with Parsi caps on our skulls. It was a huge funeral, the pride of our neighbourhood. In Ashish's house there was tremendous organization. The women came in shifts for four days and set up a hearty wail. The men, Parsis, Muslims, Hindus, Christians, all who had benefited or hoped to benefit from the ice factory and the future tractor factory, came and sat on the hundreds of chairs provided for the occasion in the compound of the ice factory and the street outside it. It was the central event of the neighbourhood. On the day when the body was to be carried away, the crowds were uncontrollable. My grandfather and all my aunts and cousins attended.

In the passageway between the house and the factory, Samson's men changed into their body-carrying outfits. When the khandias, the men of carrion, emerged from the alley, there would be wailing and gnashing of teeth in the congregation. We, Ashish's friends, sat on the rows of chairs outside the room in which the dead body was being prayed over for the last time. We would be called in at a particular point in the ceremony to file past the body in the room and touch its feet and mutter a prayer. Ashish came and joined us. His father came out several times from the ceremony with the air of a busy foreman.

Samson looked proud. He was wearing a white muslin tunic and white pyjamas. He led his team of body-carriers as if they were olympic athletes. Their hour had come.

The next day it was business as usual in the Chowk. Kolmi, who hadn't attended the funeral, was explaining the importance of it to the traffic policeman. Two days later Ashish was back in the Chowk with a black armband on his laundered sleeve, expecting the sympathy of all who passed him.

When he came into the cafe and sat at our table, people said how clearly and beautifully the head priest had intoned his prayers. Kolmi came over to our table and spoke to Ashish.

'If I was your father, he said, 'I'd demand reduced rates for the number of lines those bastards of priests dodged. They left huge gaps. How do you expect a soul to go to heaven with all those gaps?'

Then Samson came in.

'Your father is very charitable,' he called to Ashish, out loud so that the rest of the cafe could hear. 'He gave each of us twenty rupees. For carrying his bloody mother. Weighs more than two blocks of his behnchod ice.'

The cafe was stunned. All heads turned to Samson and Ashish.

'That's more than you ever got before,' Ashish said.

'She was as heavy as a horse,' Samson said. 'Twenty rupees is charity, not payment. What does your dad think we are?

Does he think we're made of water like his ice blocks? We have to eat, you know.'

Ashish got up and left the cafe. We heard that Samson had expected at least a hundred rupees for doing that job.

'You Parsis can rot,' Samson announced to the Sachapir cafe when Ashish had gone. 'I'm not lifting people who've got fat on other people's sweat for twenty rupees.'

Samson was true to his word. He gave up carrying the bodies of the rich. He would only accept commissions from the fire temple to carry the bodies of the poor and the destitute for which he was paid a very small fee out of charity funds.

It was rumoured that men had to be imported from Bombay that year to break the strike that Samson had imposed on the other carriers.

Samson hung around the Chowk for a few months getting poorer and more ragged. He carried trays of bread for the bakery and then he went to work, grim-faced and without apology, lifting blocks of ice for Ashish's factory.

Years later, when I had left Poona, and Ashish had established himself with his father's money as a regular bookie on Poona Racecourse, a friend wrote to me to say that Samson was dead. He had graduated from working at the ice factory to being a supervisor of labour at the tractor factory which Ashish's dad had opened in Pimpri. His funeral, I'm told, was massive. Larger than any the neighbourhood had ever known. It took eight men to lift his body. Till the day he died he was called Samson, even though he had shaved his head bald when he went to work for the ice factory and a regular wage.

III

Black Dog

Trouble started with the first edition of the *Synagogue Spotlight*. It was so called because across Sachapir Street, one corner down from Sarbatwalla Chowk, ran Synagogue Street. At the end of this street was the building from which it got its name, a red-brick edifice with long glass windows and a tall brooding tower which even the pigeons who infested every eave for miles around, shunned. There were no Jews in our neighbourhood, so why the Synagogue was where it was no one could say. On Saturdays the Jewish community of the town gathered for services there. The rest of the week the large compound, overrun with weeds, with a dead well of bitter water in the corner, was deserted.

We could see the tower from all over the neighbourhood. It looked down on us. That was probably the reason Mr Minocher Toot chose to mount his scandalous metaphorical spotlight on top of it. The first edition caused some excitement in the Chowk. It contained all the gossip and filth and rumour that had circulated around the Parsi community in the previous month. The lead article on the first page said that the priests at the fire temple were not serving the dead or the living very well. They were turning up to funerals drunk and sitting through the night's prayers without the fear of God, dodging whole passages of prayers to get them over and done with. On one occasion, the article said, two of the priests had fallen asleep and had to be woken by the bereaved relatives of the dead person.

The second front page article said that Parsi girls had been seen holding hands and walking in Empress Gardens with non-Parsi boys. A college girl of the neighbourhood (the *Spotlight* didn't mention names) 'had been seen returning from her so-called studies in the company of a negro boy,' some foreign student, who was actually attempting to sing Hindi love songs to her. Did the parents of this girl know about this? Was this the point of educating the young men and women of our community?

'Who printed this rot?' Kolmi asked.

'Non-Parsis from the City,' Samson said. 'It's Minocher Toot's little rag. He's trying to be all holy in this paper and giving it to Hindus and Muslims to print, the swine.'

Samson's guess was accurate. The first edition didn't say who had put the *Spotlight* together, but on the second page of the paper an advertisement appeared. It was a giveaway. The ad said that Dr Minocher Toot, famous inventor, philanthropist and industrialist, was offering the public shares in his esteemed firm. People who contributed large sums could hope to become partners of Dr Toot and take a hand in Poona's Industrial Revolution.

'You see what the old crook is trying on now?' Kolmi asked. 'Some poor goat to the slaughter. Toot is the sultan of fraud, the king of all takers of other people's money.' From Soli Kolmi it was a rare compliment.

In our neighbourhood, 'MT Technologies' was well-known. Toot lived a few doors down from the Chowk and the board which announced his industries hung outside his house. When we were toddlers our aunts and mothers would send us round to Toot's place to ask him to repair the spring of a mousetrap or to sharpen a knife on the grinding wheel in his 'factory'.

The factory was on his back verandah. At the time the first edition of the *Spotlight* emerged, his business was making ladies' hand fans out of old film that he'd bought cheap. The rolls were cut into strips, stapled together and nailed on to bamboo handles. The Chowk gossips said that he'd borrowed six hundred rupees from some gullible fool to set this venture up and every anna of it had gone down the drain because the officials from the municipality had examined the factory and declared the film a fire hazard.

Khatu Toot, Minocher's eldest son, retold the story of the film fans in the Chowk. The fire precaution fellows were all bribe-takers, he said, and his father, being an honest man working for the good of the industrial revolution, had refused to pay their blackmail. Those fire fellows had better watch out because he, Khatu, was going to take revenge.

It was difficult to believe anything that Khatu said. He was a lanky youth with braces on his teeth. His clothes were always unfashionable. He wore broad flapping trousers, tightly buckled on to his chest with a plastic belt. Even though he was a few years older than my friends and I were and was going through college when we were still at school, we took our cue from Kolmi and Samson and the regulars and treated Khatu and his threats of murder against his father's enemies as a joke.

In the second edition of the *Spotlight,* Toot came out more clearly as the author. This edition was all about the persecution that citizens were suffering in the neighbourhood. The front page had two stories. The first was about the destruction of mango trees by the wayward youths of the neighbourhood.

Its headline said 'STOP TINAGE TERROR'. The article said that some parents in the neighbourhood, who had no doubt earned their riches through fraud, deceit and bribery, had taken to buying airguns for their 'tinage' male offspring. This was a dangerous development, because these airguns were not toys, they were weapons of terror. In the recent past the writers and editors of the *Spotlight* had noted with alarm and anger that these so-called toys were being used by these so-called boys for shooting lead pellets into mangoes which hung from the trees of unsuspecting neighbours. These lead pellets were poisonous. The scientific researches of Mr Toot's laboratory had revealed further that the angle at which the pellets entered the mangoes was such that it was proved beyond doubt that these so-called boys must be getting encouragement from malicious and jealous neighbours who allowed them to clamber over their roofs to get closer to the mangoes to damage them. The article said that legal action would be taken.

The article was a giveaway. The only mango tree in th neighbourhood which bore any fruit belonged to Minocher Toot himself. Everyone in the neighbourhood knew that for the last two seasons the mangoes had been used f target practice by Ashish's younger brother and his gang.

'Your father can't take anyone to court for that,' Kolmi said with great authority to Khatu Toot. 'If your father has one more case to answer you'll have to move your family to the law courts and sleep on charpoys outside.'

'Too many people cheat my father and shoot his mangoes,' Khatu said.

'I thought his mangoes got shot off in the Second World War, when he was a stretcher-bearer,' Samson said.

Khatu ignored the remark. 'The people of this neighbourhood can't stand his genius. Too much jealous people here, always burning, burning with jealousy.'

'Why doesn't your father invent armour plating for his mangoes?' Shahid asked.

Kolmi tapped the edition of the *Spotlight* which lay on the marble-topped cafe table.

'And this dog that's bothering him. He'd better not get on the wrong side of that dog. You'd better warn your father not to write anything about that leg-raising mongrel.'

We all knew what Kolmi meant. The second article on the front page was all about the Black Dog. It was owned by a blind man who lived in the temple charity buildings on the corner of Sachapir and Synagogue Streets. It was a big black dog with a mangy coat and very bad manners. Some people called it Bonzo and others called it Moti and Prince, but its master called it 'Black Dog'. He would shout for it when it was foraging in the gutters outside, 'Black Dog, you don't hear your pap now?'

Dog and master were despised in the neighbourhood. The *Spotlight* article said: 'There are several peoples who kip and tend viscuous pets in our fair neighbourhood. This is not domesticated pets. It is wild animals in disguise. This is very bad practice and unconvenient also.

'Now in English papers we can read how lots of blind peoples keep trained dogs and hounds to help cross road and fetch newspapers in mouth and other such things. This is very good. But in our poor country, where industrial revolution is not even taken place, people are keeping any dirty dog to create open nuisance and do its excretions in other neighbours' garden.

'The *Spotlight* says let blind mens have trained dogs but not jungle dogs.'

The article said nothing about the Chowk's blind man. Even Minocher Toot knew that, disliked as he was, the blind man attracted a certain amount of sympathy. The article could have gone on to criticize the blind man for spitting at passers-by and swearing for half an hour at a stretch at the footsteps he heard outside his door. He had other bad habits. In the hot season he would throw buckets of water out of his front door on to the pavement to cool the flagstones, without warning anyone who might be passing. It was said that he had gone blind through drinking methylated spirits and French polish, and that in the British days when good liquor was available.

Once a week a cleaning woman went into his house to ensure that he had enough food and to wash his clothes. Every two or three months a barber would turn up with an old leather bag and the blind man would sit on a chair on the pavement outside his door and have himself shaved and his straggly black locks shorn. The dog would sit next to the chair. As children we used to gather round and watch the operation and listen to the blind man swearing every time the clipping machine bit his scalp or pulled his hair. Once the machine jammed and the barber started heaving at it. The blind man jumped up and began screaming that he was being murdered and Black Dog went wild, prancing about and biting the barber in the crotch. The neighbours came out and persuaded the barber to finish the half-done job and to return in two months' time. The blind man cooled the dog down and kicked him.

In the Chowk there was a myth about this black dog. People said it led a charmed life. Samson said it was because of the white spot on its forehead. Ashish insisted that his brother's airgun pellets bounced off its mangy coat.

It was a legend which gathered momentum through all sorts of coincidences. Once when two thieves broke into the blind man's house, they got hold of the dog and tied it up with rope and clamped its muzzle with a belt from the blind man's trousers. They took what they could find andwere making their way across Sarbatwalla Chowk when the traffic lights in the centre of the crossing collapsed and hit one of them on the head. The people who came to his assistance saw that the loot he was carrying contained old porcelain vases and a gold ring which Kolmi identified as the blind man's. People said it was because of the dog. They shouldn't have tied up the dog.

There were other stories about the dog's power. The blind man would walk him once or twice a week to the sugarcane juice shop at the corner of Synagogue Street. One day when he had settled himself in the shop, which was no more than a couple of benches under a canvas roof, with a mangling machine for the cane, two young men arrived on their Lambretta. They were called Naval and Billy and were known to us as bad boys, not regulars of the Chowk but part of the Main Street mob who were richer and owned motorcycles.

Shahid and I were in the shop and watched these two walk in. Black Dog sat at the blind man's feet and every now and again the blind man dipped his finger in the white-foamed glass and allowed him to lick it.

'How are you doing, juniors?' Naval said to Shahid and me. He and Billy sat down, ordered two glasses of juice each, and began lighting cigarettes.

Suddenly Naval got up from his bench and went over to the blind man.

'Sahebji,' he said. 'Do you know me?'

'Sahebji,' the blind man replied and his face assumed its questioning expression, mouth half open and eyes blinking. 'Who's that? No, sir, your voice is familiar, but. . .I can't, no I can't place it. I'm a blind.'

'It's your long lost son,' Billy said.

Naval raised his hand, motioning Billy to be quiet.

'We need your help.'

'Yes, maybe,' the blind man said. 'What help? Who the hell are you? I'm a blind man, what help can us blinds give?'

'Don't be an actual pathetic,' Naval said. 'You've been here for the last two minutes haven't you?'

'I know your voice,' the blind man said. He was smiling uncertainly. 'You must know I come here and sit for hours on Friday.'

'Five minutes ago there was an accident on this corner. Now you're a witness. Will you come and tell the court what you saw?'

The blind man fumbled at his feet to feel Black Dog.

'Look, please leave me alone,' he said.

'Leave the guy alone, yaar, Naval,' Shahid said.

At this point Billy got up and crossed to where we were sitting.

'Who asked you to meddle in this?'

'I don't want to,' Shahid said. Billy was six feet two inches tall and had a reputation for being one of the college weightlifters.

'Why do you want to interfere with a blind man?' I asked.

'I'd like to interfere with your sister,' Billy said.

He went over to where Naval was standing in front of the blind man. He must have thought that we weren't worth bothering about.

'So you refuse to be a witness?' Billy asked.

Naval started to laugh. 'I bet he sits here to watch all the girls wiggling past.'

'I please you to leave me alone.'

Black Dog began to growl deep in his stomach.

'See here, blindey, you better hold on to your doggy or we'll put his eyes out.'

Billy thought that was a great gag. They were both laughing.

'Eh, blindey, have you seen the Sophia Loren picture at the Empire? I bet you enjoyed it, all the big tits and hairy armpits.'

'What do you think he does for a go?' Naval asked.

'I hear he has a cleaning woman coming in. He must be giving her one. Oi, does she charge blinds extra?'

'Please leave me alone, have some shame,' the blind man said.

'I don't suppose she gives it to him, or he'd be boasting about it. You know these blinds,' Naval said.

It was Billy who turned his attention to the dog. He prodded its guts with his toe.

'He probably does it with the dog.'

'Is it a female dog?' Naval asked. They were in fits of laughter.

Then Naval did the fatal thing. He leaned over, held Black Dog's muzzle and grabbed his back leg. The dog whimpered.

'It's a male dog,' Naval said. 'He probably gets at it from the back. You know these blinds.'

'I beg you to leave my dog alone,' the blind man said.

'Leave your dog alone? Why don't you leave him alone? Quite, quite shameless. I'd rather be dead than have it off with a dog. He probably did it before he went blind. God punishes the wicked.'

'Please leave us alone,' the blind man said and fumbled with the edge of the bench in an effort to stand up.

'You think you're damn smart, teasing a blind man, don't you?' Shahid said.

'You'll have enough time to think how smart you are in the hospital, so you'd better shut your gob,' Billy said.

They'd finished their juice. They cursed and abused the stall-keeper and spat ice all over the floor.

'You call this sugarcane juice? Filthy ice water.'

'They are bad boys,' the blind man said after he'd heard their scooter start up and move off. He dug in his pocket for change to pay for his drink. He didn't want to sit there any longer.

'Old man, leave it, I'll pay,' I said. I felt guilty, though neither Shahid nor I could have done much to stop the older boys.

'They shouldn't have touched the dog. I don't mind them having a little fun with me. Now I'm blind and that's my fate and bless God or curse his mother, I have to fumble my way, but the dog, what did he do to them? Black Dog hasn't done anything to them. My sweet little Black Dog.' He patted the dog into motion.

'We should take a gang from the Chowk and show those bastards,' Shahid said on our way home.

Two days later the news hit the Chowk. Naval died while riding his scooter on the high roads to the south of Poona. A truck ran him off a cliff while he was riding with a girl towards the meadows and ravines at the top of the knot of mountains called Katraj Ghat. Kolmi had heard the story in Main Street. The girl, who survived the accident, swore that the truck belonged to a firm called Dog Star Refrigeration. It wasn't a firm that operated in Poona. No one had heard the name before.

Nothing happened to Billy. Not immediately. A few years later he had two operations for cataracts in his eyes. People said he was too young to have developed cataracts. When the news got around, someone, thinking of Naval who was dead and mourned, recalled that Billy too had messed with the dog.

It was after Naval's death that the dog got worse. It dug up the garden of MT Technologies. The blind man fell ill and the dog took to wailing and howling at night. Khatu complained loud and long to the Chowk.

The third edition of the *Spotlight* turned to the subject. The headline of the article was 'THE NUISANCE OF VICIOUS ANIMALS'. It had been written with the assistance of someone who could write clearer English than Minocher.

Khatu had some pretensions to being a reader of good English books. For a year he'd carried around a dog-eared copy of *The Hound of the Baskervilles*. Now the article compared Black Dog and the bloodthirsty pets of some citizens in the neighbourhood to the wailing dogs in the Sherlock Holmes story.

'This is Khatu's work,' Kolmi said. 'His father can't write so good English. Khatu is nearly finished his BSc and he's always walking around with Shakespeare's novels.'

'This fellow is finished, yaar,' Shahid said. 'This is like signing your own death warrant. Look what Khatu has written: "Hound nuisance growing daily. Only people who are capable of tending to pets should be allowed to keep them. How can a sick blind man prevent his animal from fouling others' gardens?"'

When Khatu came in Shahid said, 'No wonder bad luck is following you like an arse follows an animal.'

'Why don't you write how your father swindled the chemists by trying to sell them cotton wool substitute made out of mashed paper?' Kishan asked.

Khatu ignored the question.

'Found a job yet?' Dara asked, sensing that he was uncomfortable at this turn of the conversation.

The whole Chowk knew that Khatu had been looking for employment since he got his BSc certificate in Chemistry. The others who'd passed out of college had all found something or other, but Khatu sat day after day in the Sachapir cafe filling in application forms and looking at the advertisements in the newspapers. 'Apply, apply and no reply,' Khatu would say, and carry on with his forms.

'Now you'll never get anything. The dog is a jinx.'

But soon after that article appeared, Khatu did get a job. He passed through the Chowk on his way to the interview which was in the City. He was wearing an old jacket that his father had worn in the thirties and he mopped his sweating face with a large white handkerchief. We wished him good luck. That evening he came back to the Kayani beaming, and he bought us all a round of double char and cakes. We drank the health of the Imperial Tobacco company and its new field officer.

'Stiff competition, men,' Khatu said, 'but plenty of scope in this job, plenty.'

'What do you have to do?' Shahid asked.

Khatu was a little reluctant to say.

'Purchase for foreign export,' was his reply.

Khatu was beside himself. The Chowk knew that the Toot family were depending on him to revive their fortunes. Ever since the fan business had been declared a fire hazard by the municipality, Minocher Toot's creditors had closed in. We had watched the bailiffs move out all the furniture the Toots owned and seen Khatu's mother crying and striking her forehead on their verandah. Nothing was left, Khatu had told us. Nothing except old clothes and discarded film. They'd even taken his younger brother's football boots and the family's primus stove.

'Now we can buy it all back,' Khatu said. 'My father is not discouraged. If I can give him two months' salary, he's going to make blinds for windows out of the film. He's invented a new fire-proof liquid plastic.'

He boasted to the Chowk that Imperial had bought him a new bicycle and paid him a month's salary in advance. The next day he appeared in the Chowk in new shoes, carrying a black leather brief-case. He told us that soon he would have a van, it was being sent for his exclusive use from Bombay.

It was some weeks before we discovered what Khatu actually did. He spent time away from the Chowk, cycling to remote villages, taking trains into the countryside around the town. Dara brought the story back. He had sighted Khatu at Poona railway station goods yard, bossing a few men who were loading cages onto a goods train. 'Monkeys, yaar, the man is selling monkeys to the whites.'

It was all over the Chowk. Khatu's job had nothing to do with tobacco. He had been hired to contact trappers who would catch and cage monkeys and he was in charge of shipping them to some Head Office in Bombay from where they would be sent to Europe for dissection and medical experiments.

When he appeared in the Chowk, people began referring to him as 'Hanuman', the god of the monkeys. It made him very unpopular. Not that there was too much sympathy for monkeys in our neighbourhood. The business smacked of slavery, of the delivery of innocents to those who would maim and kill. Khatu seemed to us to have become the representative of the unacceptable practices of foreign companies who got Indians to do their dirty work for them.

Khatu fancied himself as a bit of an expert on monkeys and their diseases. He acquired sets of injections which put monkeys to sleep and packs of drugs which tested them for rabies and he boasted that he was the dispenser of poisons and darts and nets and trappers' devices imported straight from Canada.

'Have you heard about the man who died from monkey bite?' Shahid asked Khatu. 'It seems this man had shot the monkey's mate for raiding his orchard and two years later the monkey came back and sucked all his blood.'

Khatu ignored our animosity. More and more wooden cages left Poona railway station for the lethal beyond. Khatu became somewhat prosperous. The van he had boasted about arrived and he took driving lessons. From the money he earned, Khatu bought back for his father the tools of the old inventor's trade. It was said in the Chowk that old Toot was back in business and would be looking for new partners to swindle. We looked forward to the next edition of the *Spotlight*.

When it emerged, there was another attack on Black Dog in it. This time we agreed that the attack was totally justified. Black Dog had overstepped the mark. The *Spotlight* needn't have told the story because everyone in the neighbourhood knew every detail of it.

What had happened was that a distant relative of the Toot family, an old lady who lived on her own six doors away from the blind man in the temple charity buildings, had fallen down her back stairs and died. The whole neighbourhood dutifully turned out for the funeral. Minocher Toot himself took charge of all the arrangements. Khatu persuaded Samson to come off his body-carrying strike and do the family a favour because the lady was very poor. Samson had volunteered his whole team to give the dead woman a dignified bearing through the town for no payment. She was well-known to us because when we were younger she would call us off the streets and give us bhakras which she'd fried herself, and which smelt and tasted of her flat and her rancid oil and her kindness.

Now one of the ceremonies that Parsis have to undergo when they are dead, is being sniffed by a dog. My grandfather told me the origin of it. He said that the pulse and heartbeat and so on were unreliable indicators of death. The ancient Parsis, even before they came over from Persia in the eighth century, knew better. They would get a dog to sniff the body of the supposedly dead person. If there was any life left in the body, the dog would smell it out and its tail would begin to wag. If the body was indeed dead flesh, the tail of the dog would remain tucked between its hind legs, the final flag. Then the khandias could confidently carry it away.

The dog used for this purpose in our neighbourhood was called Rustum. It was constantly tied to a rope and kept in the back shed of the fire temple. Rustum was white with black spots and was quite well groomed. But he was perpetually depressed. Being toted around to funerals by Samson and his crew wasn't much of a job. We didn't wonder

45

that he was depressed. I had seen Rustum a few times, playing in the fire temple garden or being led by Samson's men to funerals. He had his tail between his legs perpetually. He didn't seem like a very reliable barometer of death.

The blind man, who lived six doors down from the Toot relative whose funeral it was, didn't ever go to funerals. On the day of her funeral, just to show he didn't care, he let Black Dog out to forage for food wherever he could find it.

From our gate on Sachapir Street, we watched the proceedings. Rustum was brought out. A young boy in a Parsi skull cap held on to him. Rustum looked as though he wanted to run away. His expression under the black patch over his left eye, was one of extreme misery. He knew he was being held there to be trotted off to smell yet another dead body. His tail was where it always was.

Black Dog was oblivious to the seriousness of Rustum's purpose. He gambolled up and down the street and finally caught sight of Rustum standing, rope around his depressed neck, in his territory. He went up and started sniffing under Rustum's tail. The boy in the skull cap tried to shoo him away. Several people at the funeral came and tried to get Black Dog to go away, finally threatening him with a stone. But Black Dog wouldn't move. He didn't like Rustum and he growled low in his throat and bared his teeth in a nasty grin.

A stone caught Black Dog on the head and then all hell was let loose. The chanting of prayers was interrupted by snarling and snapping and the whining of poor Rustum. Black Dog had bitten him in the neck and in the flank before being finally driven away by Samson with a stick.

Rustum did his job. He was dragged, bleeding and whining, into the funeral chamber with his tail firmly between his legs and no one could tell whether he was depressed because he smelt death or because his backside was raw.

That was the story as it appeared in the *Spotlight*. For once it won the sympathy of all who read it.

'She might even have been alive, but now we'll never know,' Khatu said.

'You should have brought one of your monkeys to sniff her,' Kolmi said.

'My father is right. Something has to be done about that dog.'

'But no one is going to do it. That dog is more powerful than religion,' said Dara.

A few days after the funeral, we were sitting on the steps of Messrs P. S. Chindy and Sons, the local sandalwood merchants. The street was deserted. It must have been about two in the afternoon when everyone who wasn't working took a snooze. Black Dog came trotting out of Minocher Toot's gate. It crossed the street towards the blind man's house and its back legs staggered, as though unable to hold its weight. Then as we watched, it vomited. It made a circle or two in the street and bared its teeth and collapsed. We went up to the dog and Kishan prodded it with a stick. Its muscles twitched and its tongue fell out of its mouth onto the road.

'It's dead,' Khushroo said.

We examined it warily and dragged it by its hindlegs on to the pavement. We went and knocked on the blind man's door. He came out of his house and we led him to Black Dog. He fell to his knees and began to stroke the mangy coat of the animal. He put his ear to the dog's chest and he hugged it.

'Your poor papa is calling you,' he said. 'Wake up, Black Dog, wake up. It's not dark, it's daylight, wake up.'

He was on his knees. The drops trickled out of the marble hardness of his eyes.

'You left your papa all alone, your blind papa.'

'He's dead,' I said. We shuffled our feet.

'He's only sleeping. He often sleeps,' the blind man said. 'Sometimes he can't tell night from day. You don't know his ways.'

'He came on to the road and behaved like he was mad,' I said. 'Now he's dead. He vomited.'

'Shut your filthy mouth, you urchin,' the blind man said. 'My boy is sick, he's just sick.' He cradled the dog's head in his lap. 'Black Dog is very sick.'

We knelt by the man and his dog. He was right. The dog was still alive. A shiver passed through its body and its legs stiffened and relaxed a few times. The blind man's hands clutched the dog's muzzle and his face looked up at us for assistance and advice.

'Take him to the vet,' Khushroo said.

'I don't know about the vet. Where is the vet?'

'We'll stop you a rickshaw, he'll take you. Have you got five rupees?'

'What's money?' the blind man said. 'It's the dirt of your hand. I have five hundred rupees.'

We stopped the next rickshaw and explained to the driver. The blind man was bundled in carrying Black Dog. The driver churned the accelerator and, turning on two wheels, headed for the city.

'He was there waiting,' Kolmi said the next day when the death of Black Dog was being discussed.

'Who?'

'That bastard Khatu. A real son of his father. He must have taken some of his English monkey poison and poisoned the dog.'

'So why did he go to the vet's?'

'Why do you think? You think he wanted the whole world to know that he poisoned the dog? He's a sly one. He told the blind man that he was there making monkey talk with the vet. He must have paid the vet fifty rupees to shut his mouth. Anyway, the next time someone wants to poison his wife, he can go to Khatu.'

'The vet told the blind man that Black Dog had died from eating rubbish from the gutter. Can you believe that? That dog was brought up in the gutter,' Samson said and he spat, right there in the restaurant. 'Khatu shouldn't have done it. He'll have to pay for messing with that dog.'

The blind man cried publicly for three days. He left the doors of his house open and sat on his doorstep and cried for Black Dog in regular shifts. He cursed and swore. After the third day he shut his house and went into silent and solitary mourning.

On the fourth day the MT Technologies of Dr Minocher Toot caught fire. The film, the new gadgets in the back-verandah factory, the monkey drugs, all went up in the blaze. Everyone in the neighbourhood gathered on the street to see the fire, all except the blind man. The insurance company told Toot the next day that they wouldn't pay a pice: they said he had been warned.

IV

Boomerang

The school I was sent to was some miles from the Chowk in a part of town recognized as the habitation of the Indian Army. The school stood on a hill and all around it were quiet streets of bungalows which would have been occupied by British officers in the old days but had now been handed over to Majors and Colonels from the Indian Army Medical Corps and the Bombay Sappers and Miners. Wooden signs on the gate-posts told people to keep away, to beware of the dog that protected the unkempt garden beyond the overgrown hedge.

Those of us who went from the Chowk and its environs to that particular school went by bicycle, racing each other breathlessly up the slopes, out of the mire of our neighbourhood, beyond Main Street to the education which was reserved, as our teachers constantly reminded us, for the sons of officers and gentlemen. Most of us 'townwallahs' went there because our parents saved to send us. It was a school that prided itself on being several cuts above the Jesuit school in the marketplace, the Parsi school to which most of the boys from our neighbourhood went or the municipal schools to which the poor and the working class sent their children and where those who were expelled from the other schools landed up.

Our Headmaster found the opportunity each morning at assembly to remind us in some small way that he was in the business of training future soldiers and men of character and determination. The school had a tradition dating back to 1864, he said. It had been founded by British bishops and though the captains and the kings had departed, the school would continue to train boys in the hard-living Christian tradition.

The boarders at the school, sons of army and naval officers, sons of businessmen from Bombay and civil servants from all over India, accepted that the bad food, the whippings, the unflagging concentration on running from one place to the next to build stamina, the dormitories which were old converted barracks and leaked in the monsoon, the ex-army British sergeants who had stayed behind in India to train us, were all part of this character-building process.

The Headmaster didn't like the day scholars. We were tolerated because we brought in a certain amount of money, because we helped swell the numbers and mainly, I think, because some government regulation stipulated that a Poona school couldn't function without boys from Poona. He used to refer to us as 'the natives'. In his estimation we were just one rung above the people he referred to as 'bazaar urchins' and the 'blighted, benighted of India'. His knowledge, such as it was, was respected; his cane was feared. He was a sentimentalist who tried to inspire 'his boys' with a softness for silly traditions. Several times at assembly he would display a glass phial attached to his key chain and tell the school that it contained the mud of his 'alma mater', the school he had attended as a boy. He had gathered this memento from the path where his school mates had walked.

He was an enthusiast for religion and made us pray with our eyes shut and drilled us to sing hymns, the meanings of which were a greater puzzle to me than the prayers I said at home in the dead language of the Parsi scriptures. 'As pants the hart for cooling streams, When heated in the chase', was to me like those funny cut-out transfers in which the head doesn't match the body, because the words didn't seem to fit together. I thought, till I was much older, that the lines had something ungrammatical to do with trousers and chests and fire and 'chase' suggested to me some kind of old stove.

Amongst those of us who came from the Chowk and the lowly neighbourhoods of the town, there was a tacit under-standing, a rejection of 'character', 'tradition', 'discipline' and gentlemanliness. We had as much use for these as we had for test tubes of mud from the school drive. We lived a sort of double life, hanging about the Chowk in the evenings drinking single char, shedding our maroon ties and white shirts, wandering about in gangs, shooting pigeons with deadly catapults or with .177 airguns, organizing kite-flying tournaments, bicycling to the filthy river for a nocturnal swim. School seemed to prove that work was one thing and living another.

The boarders lived a dreary life with a pitiable routine. They were paraded for breakfast, paraded for lunch and dinner, paraded for baths and study and paraded to be inspected before they left school once a fortnight for a few hours to visit bounded precincts of the town. The Chowk was out of bounds for them. They could only descend as far as Main Street and could only go to the two English picture houses. Doom would follow if they ventured into the 'native' enclaves. Imposed by some Englishman who had headed the school, the rules were a sorry imitation of the law the Tommies lived by and defied when they were garrisoned in Poona.

Between the boarders and the day scholars there was constant rivalry. Each side had its own strengths. We had bicycles which they yearned to borrow. They had access to the scandal and dirty stories about the masters' wives. They were good at running and boxing and football and the best of them could probably beat the hell out of the best of us in hand to hand combat. But we had the knife men, the gang men, the boys who treated self-defence as a necessity of life rather than a sport. We also had access to new clothes and, most important of all, to food cooked at home.

Terry Soakum was a boarder. He was a white boy and came to our class for the first time, ushered by an Anglo-Indian matron, in tears. His arrival caused a quickly quelled stir in the class. There was one other white boy at the school and there had been a third. This third was a Danish boy who spoke no English. He was the son, it was said, of a great Danish engineer who had come to Poona to set up the first penicillin factory in the suburb called Pimpri. This boy constantly smiled, was left alone by most others and came to school in a large chauffeur-driven car. He stayed a year, was of little account and disappeared when his father's expertize was no longer needed in the penicillin plant.

The other white boy was Kimber. He was the son of missionaries and had lived all his life in Poona. He behaved like the rest of us; he spoke English with our accent, he played and prayed and lied and scrapped. His only distinction was being called 'white-spunk' and wearing woollen hose, come hot summer, come monsoon, because his dad had picked up, through acquaintance with the jungle regions of India, the belief that they kept leeches off.

We gathered round the new arrival at break time. He sobbed silently as he was shown how to lock his desk and make up his time-table. Through his sobs and his wet eyes which stared at one spot, he made it known that he was from Australia, from Perth. He had cried all the way on the plane. We never thought of asking him how he'd landed up in Poona.

He was a curiosity to the rest of the school and crowds gathered to see him, as though a strange animal had been imported to the old zoo. He wasn't wearing school uniform and continued for the next few days in his blue velvet shorts and frilled silk shirt. He carried a painted boomerang with him and clutched on to it as though it was the one spar from a broken ship in the enveloping sea of the present.

The boomerang became the centre of attention after Soakum's strange accent and clothes and manners lost their initial charm. It never performed in my sight, but word reached the gang I used to circulate with that Terry Soakum could ring the school bell with it.

Our school bell consisted of a piece of railway track about a yard in length, suspended from the rafters of the dinner hall verandah. Each year the tallest boarder in the eleventh standard was entrusted with the bell-ringer's job and given a large iron bolt as a sign and instrument of office. The bolt was rattled in the groove of the rail, producing a clang that reached the most remote classroom and games group. We heard now that Soakum could ring this bell from a distance of thirty yards and catch the wooden bird as it homed back to him.

On the fourth day that Soakum was there he was summoned to the presence of our gang. Its leader was Farokh Habibulla. He was the only boy who was seventeen and was growing a moustache amongst the day scholars. The rest of us were fourteen and fifteen. He was a veteran. He had spent three years in the tenth standard because he hadn't passed his exams. He was a weightlifter. His muscles bulged out of rolled-up sleeves. He gave demonstrations of his strength by shaking the trunks of well-established trees and he always managed to speak, to teachers and to the rest of us, in a growl which seemed to come from way down in his guts.

'Send for the Australian,' he said.

A couple of the gang went to seek out the Soakum circus, the jeering bunch of third and fourth standard tykes who followed Soakum around wherever he went. In a few minutes, Soakum was brought to us.

'I hope you like India,' Farokh Habibulla said.

'I don't like the boys, they're not nice boys. In Australia. . .'

'In Australia people smell like sheep,' Haby said.

'Tell him please, to let go of my arm. It hurts,' Soakum shrieked. The gathering laughed.

Haby gave a vague signal with his eyebrows and Terry Soakum was released.

'All right, now give me that crooked stick.'

'It's a boomerang.'

'How much does it cost.'

'You can't buy it in rupees. It costs pounds, shillings and pence.'

'That's all right then. If I can't buy it I'll take it.'

Haby stretched his hand out. Soakum quickly held the boomerang behind his back. Haby wiggled his fingers. Two boys detached themselves from our gang and prised the boomerang out of Soakum's fingers.

'My dad gave it to me,' Soakum said. Haby was examining the shaft. It was varnished and the grain of the wood ran in a curved pattern around its angle. The boomerang had blue and yellow patterns painted on it.

'Can you make it come back if you throw it? I hear you're gassing too much about its comings and goings.'

'He can't,' some little boys shouted. 'He can only polish it on his pants.'

'I can make it come back,' Haby said.

'You?' Soakum said with unconcealed contempt. 'Only abos and bushrangers can use it properly.'

'If I can, I'll keep it,' Haby said.

He stepped out of the ring of boys and walked authoritatively to clear ground.

'You don't hold it like that,' Soakum said.

Haby was holding the boomerang by its middle. He knew everyone was staring at him. He weighed the instrument like a man putting the shot. Then he held it at knee height.

'If it comes back, I'll keep it,' Haby said.

'It won't come back for you,' Soakum said.

Haby laughed and threw the boomerang vertically in the air. It hung for a moment like a seagull taking the current, and swooped back downward. Haby ran a few steps and caught it.

Everyone except Soakum laughed.

'It's mine now,' Haby said. 'I've proved the laws of nature.'

'Give it back,' Soakum said stepping forward to grapple with Farokh.

'Getting nasty, eh?' Haby said and holding the boomerang with both hands now he raised his knee and cracked it in two. He handed the pieces back to Soakum.

'Australians are all daft,' he said.

Then for the first time we heard the cry that was to become famous in school. Soakum began howling.

'Ooooooooooooo,' he sang out. His face turned red and rich tears dropped from his wide eyes.

Some people laughed and the smaller boys, feeling bold, kicked him from behind and ran away. I felt sorry for Soakum, but feeling sorry for people wasn't done in our school.

In the months that followed, the velvet-clad boy disappeared. Soakum's two sets of uniform cottons were issued to him and became tatty and ragged. His neat hair grew in tangled blond locks which the masters delighted in pulling when he gave the wrong answers, as he invariably did in class. The matron ordered that he have a crew cut. His shoes gave way to a pair of canvas sneakers from which his toes soon sprouted. He picked up the ways of the filthiest boarders and stuffed buttered buns from breakfast into his shirt when he could steal them. The butterfly had turned caterpillar.

The school got to know, when Soakum didn't pack his trunks as the rest of the boarders did the day before the holidays, that Australia was far away and worse, that Soakum's father had stopped sending money or fees to the school. Terry Soakum had been abandoned in India. After several unanswered letters, the Headmaster had sent Soakum to be interviewed by the Anglican mission which paid the school fees and pocket money of the very poor Christians.

At first Soakum cried and tried to hide the shame of being abandoned, but in a term's time he acquired the shamelessness of the very poor. He was flogged publicly at assembly three times for stealing the belongings of others boys in his dormitory. He began to be known as a 'chokrá boy', a street urchin, and lived up to the role by learning all the taunts and abuse that street urchins used. Soakum became the closest thing to an Indian derelict that a white boy could be.

He got a reputation for being a howler. At the end of each month the boys in all classes were given tests in each subject. The marks were added up and the sum divided to give each boy an average on his report card and a place and rank in class. At the end of the month the Headmaster visited each class in turn. His entry would be signalled by a flurry of activity and then complete silence. The black-gowned, cane-carrying figure would carefully pick up the register. The report cards would be handed round and then the names of those who had failed in the monthly tests would be read out.

The reward for each subject that a boy failed was one cut of the cane on the bum. In the junior classes the beating was handed out in front of the class. After the ninth standard, when most of the boys were fourteen, the failures were invited by the Headmaster to form a queue outside the classroom on the verandah. He would step outside and call the names one by one and the thrashings would follow. The boys who had passed would sit tight and silent and listen and thank God for brains or concentration or whatever it was that caused them to know the date of the second battle of Panipat or the real name of Gautam the Buddha.

Soakum was always left till last, because the Headmaster knew that beating him would disrupt the sequence. He would start screaming before the cane hit him, his dread mounting as the queue in front got shorter. He used to fail ten subjects at a time, bettering Habibulla who usually managed to fail six or seven.

Haby would be second to last in the queue.

He would bend down, take his strokes motionless and raise his head to ask the Head if he was finished.

He'd get two more for insolence.

Haby would stroll back into class, pretending to clean his teeth with his tongue, a device which allowed him to disguise the fact that his mouth was contorted with pain and determination not to show it. Then Soakum would begin howling in earnest, 'Ooooooooooooo', shrill and unashamed.

'You mustn't show the bastard you're scared of his stick,' Haby would advise us. 'Day scholars must show they are as tough as these leather-eating boarders.'

It was difficult to follow his advice. The pain was compelling. On the occasions when I got three cuts for bringing raw mangoes to school, or for being seen with a mob of my friends, barefoot in Sachapir Street, I had to fight myself to keep the tears back. Blinking fast always helped, though it betrayed the straight face you were trying to keep, and rubbing your mouth so that the rest couldn't see the corners curling downwards. Whenever I got beaten, I reminded myself that I mustn't be like Soakum. He was the symbol of cowardice in the school.

The one thing that took some of the pain away was the interest that the others showed in your bottom after a severe beating.

'Give us a look, let's have a look.'

You'd take your trousers down and bend for all to see. They'd pass their fingers along the ridged cuts.

'It's gone yellow, yaar. Ooophhh. Look at this men, purple.'

No one wanted to see Soakum's bum. After a beating he ran around the school grounds clutching it, howling and running in circles like a rabid dog. The teachers were used to it. They gave up demanding that he came back and sat down like the rest of the disgraced rascals. Yet it was a game to remind Soakum of the beating the next day and make him crane his neck to look over his shoulder, standing on tip-toe to examine his own backside. Sometimes the memory of it would revive his howl.

Through being a coward, Soakum turned into a bully. The frightened long to inspire fear and feed off the inspiration. Two years at our school had taught him that the best way to acquire the possessions he wanted was not to steal them from his fellow seniors, but to take them from smaller and younger boys. He used to force third standard boys to go to secluded parts of the playground with him and exchange their socks for his torn ones. He extracted shares of melon slice and coconut toffee from them. He borrowed hockey sticks by beating their owners with them. It was known that he picked on the weak and the weedy and the defenceless.

I didn't think of myself as either of these and was mortified when he picked on me. I was the second smallest boy in the class. The smallest had a younger brother who was one year behind but already five foot six inches tall. They were both boarders and lived in the same dormitory and no one harassed them. I was conscious from the day I joined that class that I wore the thickest spectacles, and had the knobbliest knees which the rest laughed at when I was asked to climb ropes in PT classes. In the early years I was used to being called 'four-eyes' but now when the boys of Sarbatwalla Chowk began to gang together, I felt a certain amount of security from membership of Haby's gang.

Soakum was after my swimming trunks. On the mornings when we had swimming, we wore our trunks under our trousers or shorts and sat in them through the lessons till it was time to go. The class would be dismissed and told to get to the baths as fast as possible. The day scholars would get on their bicycles and race each other to the pool which was a quarter of a mile away and the boarders would begin their run to be the first there. There was constant competition to be the first in the pool, so as you cycled along or ran, you began stripping yourself of your shirt and, if you could manage it, your trousers.

As the race for the pool began that day, I was the last to get my bike out of the shed and get started. As I was going through the school gate I passed Soakum. He got hold of the book carrier of my bike.

'Give us a double seat, man.'

'No, no. Why can't you run like all the other boarders?'

'Don't be such a skunk. Give us a cha-nus.'

Soakum jumped on to the back carrier. I heard his breath and felt his weight pull the bicycle to a halt.

'Come on, Dhondy. What's the matter with you, are you a TB patient?'

'I'm no good at double seat, yaar. Police will catch us, then who'll pay the fine?'

The bike had moved a few yards and it began to veer from side to side through loss of momentum.

'Soakum get off, or I'll kick you.'

'Don't fart in my face,' he said. 'If you've got lung trouble, I'll take you doubles.'

'No, it's my bike.'

Soakum got off the bike and grabbed the back of the seat with both hands. It was no good trying to get away. The others were out of sight now. I decided to let him try to carry me.

Soakum got on to the seat and I got on the carrier. He puffed and panted, standing on the pedals to force them down.

'Is this an Indian-make bike?'

'I'll give you a little dhhukka,' I said, pushing the ground with my feet.

We moved off slowly. We were going to be the last in the pool and the rest of the class would jeer. I unrolled my towel and hung it round my neck and began to get my shirt off. At least I would be in the pool before Soakum. He was panting and struggling up the hill now. I unbuttoned my shorts and was going through the gymnastics of taking them off by sliding them under me, when Soakum swerved.

'What are you doing, yaar, you're making me lose balance.'

The bike careened sideways and we both landed in the gutter.

'Look what you've done to the bike,' I said, and stood up, my shorts almost falling off. The handlebars of the bike were twisted. Soakum wasn't paying any attention. He was staring at my new trunks.

'I say, can I have those? I'll give you my trunks.'

'You off your head or what? My uncle got them from Hong Kong.'

'I think you'd better take them off and give them to me,' Soakum said, rising from the ditch and standing over me as I got the front wheel of the bike and tried to pull the handlebars straight.

'I'll give you my new catty,'

'I don't want your catty,' I said.

He took the catapult out of his shirt.

'Look at this leather on it, it's special leather, made from rhinoceros balls.'

'Don't talk bunk, yaar. I told you I don't want your catty.'

'All right then, I'll break your teeth,' he said and grabbed me by the shirt. 'Take off those swimmies.'

'Get off,' I shouted and pushed him away.

Soakum picked up a stone from the side of the road.

'You want your specs bashed into your skull? Filthy four-eyes.'

'I'm not scared of you,' I replied, trying to get my bicycle between him and me.

I bent down and picked up a stone too.

'Okay, no stones, man,' he said and dropped the one he was holding. He scowled and came right up to me. He gritted his teeth and made an ugly face and as I stared at it he pinched me on the thigh.

I pushed my elbow in his neck and he released his hold. Then he grabbed the towel from round my neck and began to run up the road.

I got on the bike and chased him. As he got to the gate of the swimming pool he picked up a stone and hurled it at me. It hit me in the chest. I was furious. I threw my bike down and chased him to the side of the pool. Then he threw my towel into the water.

'Now you can't swim either,' he said.

If the teacher hadn't been there I would have got him by the neck. I was mad. The stone hadn't hit me hard, but I was smarting from the insult. Very few boys had ever had cause to challenge me to fight. I had fought once or twice in the junior classes and emerged with my clothes torn. But this was Soakum, the biggest crybaby in the school. The rest of them had seen him throw my towel in the pool. He would go around telling the boarders that he had beaten me up. Hadn't he the sense to know that I was part of a tough gang? Of course I didn't want the protection of the gang. I had to fight this out myself. But how could I tell Haby and the rest of my friends that I wanted to fight Soakum? They'd laugh. Soakum was someone you rapped on the head, not challenged to a fight.

When we queued up after swimming I made my way next to him.

'I'll give you a kicking,' I said in a whisper.

'Come to the lowers after school,' he said. 'And bring your knife. I don't fight day scholars without a knife.'

On the way back to school I stuck with the Sarbatwalla Chowk crowd.

'Why didn't you swim?' Haby asked me.

'That bugger Soakum, he threw my towel in the pool.'

'Soakum? You let him touch your towel? You'll get a disease.'

'I'm going to fight him.'

'I'll give him one backhander and he'll go flying,' Haby said.

'I'm going to kill him myself,' I said.

'When?'

'After school today. On the lowers. He said to bring a knife. I don't have a knife.'

'Look, have this one,' one of the others said and he pulled a switchblade from his pocket. I couldn't refuse it now. I weighed it in my palm.

This thing was getting out of hand. I had never used a knife before, though I had heard fights discussed a hundred times on the Chowk. Kolmi used to tell the story of how Thomas the Boxer was knifed one procession night and how his guts lay in the street from the gash which had gone in and up and how you could see that he had eaten rice and curd for dinner.

I looked at the switchblade and turned it in my hand and tried it once or twice. I was wishing the fight wasn't anything to do with knives. I knew that if I struck out blindly with my elbow or my fist, Soakum would start howling even before I touched him. If he started that, fighting him would bring disgrace, but less disgrace than backing away from a quarrel with him would. I had to go through with it.

'Boarders never use knives,' Haby said. He looked meditative. 'Why didn't you just ask him to punch for punch?'

'Whatever he wants,' I said.

I wasn't concentrating on my afternoon lessons. Soakum sat six desks behind me. I could sense his gaze on my neck. Knife fights needed skill, not strength. Anyone could win. I wasn't going to admit to myself that I was scared, but a rush of blood under my ears and a looseness about my wrists told me I was certainly *something*. At the change of lessons an unusual silence came over the class. The maths teacher came in.

He was a middle-aged Anglo-Indian man. Like the other teachers he carried a cane in his armpit. He began each lesson by going through the drill of times tables with the class. 'Shix shixteens,' he would say with his peculiar lisp and point his cane at a boy who would have to answer. If the answer was correct, he'd move to the next boy.

'Shoakum. Nine shevens?' he asked.

Soakum was also in a daze.

'What?'

'I'll give you what! Nine shevens?'

'Uh, fifty-six.'

It was the sort of opportunity the maths teacher was always waiting for. He tucked his cane back in his armpit, and as if inviting the class to relish this absurdity with him, he began to pace up and down.

'Shoakum sheems to shay that nine shevens are fifty-shix. Fifty-shix. *Fif-tee* shix.'

'Seventy-nine,' Soakum said.

It was too late to change his mind. The maths teacher was revelling in it.

'Fifty-shix.'

'Eighty-five.'

'*Fifty*-shix.'

'Seventy-seven. Thirty-nine. Forty-eight.' Soakum was

getting frantic. 'What is it? What is it?' he asked in an audible whisper.

'Say a hundred and five,' Haby growled.

'A hundred and five,' Soakum shouted.

'Say a hundred and one,' someone said.

'Shoakum shays, nine shevens are *fif-ty*-six.' The master's pace picked up momentum. It was still deliberate, sadistic.

'Forty-nine. A hundred and forty-four. Sixty-eight,' Soakum screamed.

'Fifty-shix.'

The cane came out of the armpit and down on to Soakum's shoulder then across his face and down on the arms he held up to protect himself

'Twenty too. . .oooooooooooooooo,' came Soakum's full-throated siren wail. 'They told me, sir, they gave me the wrong answers.'

'I'll give you fifty-shix. I'll shee to your wrong anshers, you dishgrashe to Aushtralian manhood, you shquirming chokrawallah.'

Soakum ran out of the class as soon as the stick permitted him to. The master ignored his flight and went on with fractions on the board. When the bell rang for the end of school, Farokh Habibulla came up to my desk.

'Are you going to the lowers, Farrukh?'

'I'm going,' I said. 'Will you come and hold my specs?'

As I had expected, a crowd gathered. Word had got round school that there was to be a fight to the death.

I was sweating. Soakum wasn't there. Then the cry went up, 'Soakum's coming.'

Sure enough, he was coming, but he was coming in the company of the headmaster. There was a general scurry. Boys began to run to left and right. Fighting on the lowers was prohibited and spectators if caught were thrashed before participants were, for encouraging fights.

The crowd broke and ran and I stood there like an idiot for a moment or two looking at the knife in my hand. Then I ran too.

'Dhondy,' the head's voice boomed out from behind me. I stopped. The game was up. Soakum stood next to the head wiping his nose on his sleeve.

'What were you here for?'

'Fight, sir.'

'You were going to fight Soakum?'

'Yes, sir.'

'You were going to settle your differences like gentlemen through a duel?'

'Yes, sir.'

'Where are the gloves? Have your seconds run off with them?'

I didn't answer.

'Bare fists? Like hooligans, eh?'

Again I said nothing.

'Turn out your pockets, lad. I've heard some very serious allegations.'

I did as I was told. Out came my keys, two pencils, a pack of chewing gum, a couple of marbles, a piece of plastic carving and the switchknife.

'You day scholars can't fight like gentlemen, can you? Soakum told me he suspected you would bring a knife. He was prepared to have it out like a man, but you had to bring your dirty bazaar tricks into it, didn't you, Dhondy?'

Soakum stood behind the head, a faint grin on his face.

'But he. . .' I couldn't go any further.

Both Soakum and I were presented on stage to the school the next day at assembly, standing at ease, our hands clutched behind our backs.

'These boys chose to fight yesterday. One is a day scholar, one is a boarder. Both of them get the stick. One of them is a coward and the other is a sneak. Neither of these weaknesses is going to be tolerated in this school. They're not pukka. . .'

I held my knees as the cane came down and my knuckles turned white. I clutched tight and thought 'As pants the hart for cooling streams' and tried to distract my mind with figuring it out. I caught the eyes of the eleventh standard at the back of the assembly as I rubbed my backside and took my position next to Soakum. Farokh Habibullah nodded at me and smiled.

Soakum howled but this time no one so much as smirked. The incident wasn't mentioned again.

Soakum acquired a new pair of swimming trunks from no one knew where. He never bothered me again and in a few weeks we were on trading if not talking terms again.

When I returned to India after being in another country, having finished school and done with college and worked abroad for several years, I met Farokh Habibulla on the Chowk again. We talked of old times. He was in business. I was a schoolteacher. We laughed together.

'And what happened to Soakum, he didn't pass his exams did he?'

'Oh God, you won't believe this,' Farokh said. 'It was in the newspapers. He went back to Australia after school and you know what job he got?'

'Repairing boomerangs?'

'No, Farrukh. He became a professional boxer. He was fighting for the lightweight title in Melbourne last month.'

V

Dinsy

Sarbatwalla Chowk would be alive on results night, the lights on in most of the houses down the streets till well past midnight. The teenagers would keep a vigil. Once a year, every year, a carnival atmosphere, fraught with tension, would descend on the Chowk. The results of the final public school-leaving examinations would arrive in the form of newspaper boys screaming from their bicycles: 'SSCE rese-o-alts.'

Judgement day for some of us, walking about the streets nonchalantly, praying to a God if He existed. 'Let my number come up, please not a third class.' So much depended on the results. Fathers, mothers, aunts, uncles, brothers, sisters, the squad of retired teachers who ran coaching classes for the slow and the lazy, would all mingle with the regulars on the Chowk that night. Here would be Chizgar Master, king of maths, and there would sit Master Paranjpe, the man who could guarantee a pass in Physics and Chemistry at least, for twenty rupees a month.

The stalls in the alleys would do a trade in their cashew and orange flavoured liquors. The more enterprising of the bookies would have placed bets on which teenager from our neighbourhood would do best.

For six years on results night, Dinsy had hung around Uncle Frankie's with the bookies. 'Waiting to drown my sorrows, yaar,' he'd say. He had failed the exam six times.

The special edition would list the exam serial numbers of the candidates who had passed, starting with the first classes, then going on to the seconds and, overleaf, the thirds. The names of those who'd stood first overall or in the subjects that carried prizes, would be in the headlines: 'Dhondy Tops SSCE Lists', or 'Mancherji from Bishops' School Scores 90%'. Dinsy would grab the paper, spread it out on the wooden benches of Uncle Frankie's and start perusing the lists from the third class passes upwards with a faltering finger and failing hopes.

When I passed, he failed again. Passing meant the end of the school, it meant joining the ranks of the college boys and girls, it meant new clothes, celebrations with sweets the next day, a trip to the fire temple to thank God in whom a temporary belief would re-emerge.

Constant failure brought Dinsy a strange kind of youth. One year he'd be hanging around our front verandah discussing possible questions on the Geography paper with my sister. Then a year or two after that he'd be back, claiming my attention. Talk of exams became a second language with him.

'If Warren Hastings came up this time, Clive is bound to come next or Lord Cornwallis and Dalhousie, very important.' He'd flip through the 'guides' to the exams which he'd carried with him like holy writ for six or seven years. They were cheaply printed books, heavily crossed and underscored by Dinsy and his tutors. By the time he did the exams with us every line had been underlined.

Dinsy would count the reforms of this or that Indian emperor on his fingers: 'Sher Shah? He built wells and shady trees for travellers, rest houses, I forgot rest houses last time. Encouraged sports and painting, laid down the laws in codified form. Boyle's Law last time, Charles' Law next time, Artesian wells in Geography, that poem about broken livers for translation in Hindi. . .'

'You ought to go on a diet,' Kolmi told Dinsy the day after our results. 'You've got such a big body, it must be hard to pump blood up to your brain. That's why you forget so much.'

Dinsy took his failure well. He would congratulate all those who passed and be the last to leave the Kayani on results night.

He was a big man. His father was even bigger. Their fights reverberated round the neighbourhood, louder than the radio of the Sachapir Restaurant. They lived in a first-floor flat in Dastur Meher Road with four discreet white curtains on their four front windows. When the fights started, the men in the billiards saloon opposite would stop their game and take ringside streets. Dinsy's father used to hurl furniture out of the window and once or twice threw Dinsy out too.

'You're no son of mine. Your mother was stuck to the monkey god, Hanuman.'

'What's that, you horse-itch-groined bastard?'

'Can't hear me, eh? You got bania's balls in your ears?'

On one occasion when Dinsy was thrown to the pavement, he rushed into the Kayani and grabbed a bread knife from the service counter. Samson and Kolmi and whoever else was standing around fell on him and stopped him from killing his father.

After his sixth failure, Dinsy announced that he would no longer go to Chizgar's classes and that Master Paranjpe was a hoax and his guarantees were not worth a pariah dog's turd.

'You should wait for all your illegitimate children to catch up, then take the exam with them,' Kolmi said.

'You're the kind of man that would kick a corpse to show you were better,' Dinsy replied.

'Take up motor mechanics,' Kishan suggested.

'Can't. They're asking SSCE certificate, third class, for even that now.'

'Then get married to a rich woman and teach her children to do their exams. Make sure they are smarter than you or your father, though,' Kolmi said.

Dinsy became sullen after that failure. A change came over him. He bought himself new clothes and wore clean shirts and shoes instead of the Parsi slippers that we were used to seeing him in. He stopped carrying the exam guide books around. He had put stale scholarship behind him.

'So you've taken my advice?' Kolmi asked.

Dinsy didn't commit himself, but soon we got to know that it was true, he had. The rich lady that Dinsy chose was one Miss Kohla. Her first name was the plain and orthodox Parsi favourite for her generation: 'Bepsi'.

She lived at the remote end of Sachapir Street where the street crossed the City limits and became Laxmi Road, and where the houses turned to small bungalows with brick walls enclosing tiny gardens. In her garden there was an arms-width signboard which said: JOIN, JOIN, JOIN THE NEW ERA TYPING AND SHORTHAND CLASSES. EXPERT TUITION LEADING TO MONIED SALARIES.

'Twenty-seven machines,' was the word which went round the Chowk. One of her machines was particularly famous. It was a speaking attachment to a typewriter. It said, 'A S D F G, H J K L and AGAIN.'

'Where did she get this A S D F G ?' Dinsy asked.

Kishan, being a Sindhi from an ancient class of businessmen, was the expert on buying and selling in the Chowk.

'Made in the USA.'

'You mean the Ulhasnagar Sindhi Association?'

'Import, export,' Kishan said. 'Black money.'

'Her father's been dead a long time,' Dinsy volunteered.

'So? His money's not dead. It talks: A S D F G H J K L and AGAIN.'

'She's been to Japan. She must have got it from there.'

'Smugglers,' Kishan said. 'She got it from a Sindhi smuggler who is a friend of my dad. Paid him twice the money not to sell any more in Poona.'

Bepsi Kohla was hardly a figure of romance in the Chowk. She was squat with large black eyes and long hair pulled into a bun. She was known as a person from a good family, a woman of business and strategy. She kept one servant called Hukam Ali who went marketing and cooked for her. He was an old Muslim with droopy moustaches who had been with the Kohla family ever since he returned from the First World War. He had remained with Bepsi after the death of her father to serve the last of the Kohlas.

He would take time off from this service for a cup of tea in the Kayani and regale the Chowk with stories of Bepsi's classes. The Collector's daughter was turning up for shorthand lessons in the morning shift. Several businessmen, grateful to Miss Kohla for pushing their secretaries through fast typing courses in record time, had paid for her to have a holiday in Mahableshwar.

Dinsy began to question Hukam Ali. How much money did she have? How old was she really? When her father was alive, why didn't he get her married? Did she have any diseases? Was there madness in the family? False teeth? What about these relatives in Bombay?

'Why do you want to know all this? Are you spying for the rogue Mistry?' Hukam Ali would ask, evading the questions.

Mr Mistry, or 'old Mistry' as he was known to us, was the proprietor of the other typing class of the neighbourhood. His class didn't even have a name. It had but six second-hand machines which he stood on rickety tables in his front room. Old Mistry's fees for typing lessons were considerably less than Miss Kohla's. He tutored the girls of the Chowk who wanted to go into secretarial practice and he didn't have the swanky clientele from the rich suburbs of the town that Miss Kohla attracted with her advertisements. Mistry's classes lacked the door mats and neat laundered curtains and the sheer respectability of the New Era.

'Are you applying to the exam board for an honourable discharge?' Dara asked Dinsy, when he showed no signs of going back on his resolution to drop the school-leaving exams.

'Next year you can be in the headlines. Maximum failure record for this exam is six times. One more try,' Kishan said.

'My dad says that when the British used to mark the papers, they would always give something for trying hard. Not like these Maharastrian buggers,' Dinsy said. Dinsy's father consulted Chizgar Master who was the authority on boys' careers in our neighbourhood.

'Brain good, memory very bad,' was Chizgar Master's verdict. Dinsy should do something that didn't require memory. Like typing.

Dinsy chose Bepsi Kohla's class. At first he went only to the morning shift. Then he went to both, morning and afternoon. He spent his whole day at the class.

'What does she do with the money, Dinsy? Is she pickling it?'

'She is saving it to buy a man,' Kolmi said. 'Our Bepsi is no fool. Old, ugly and rich is better than young, pretty and poor. She used to push her father around. Now she only has old Hukam Ali and he's going to the service of Allah soon. Then she has to have someone to kick around. She'll get married.'

'She is not like that,' Dinsy protested. 'She is a gentle and very nice lady.'

'That's what your father thought too, Dinsy, my son, and before you were born your mother was throwing him out of the same window he uses for you now.'

Dinsy declined to challenge Kolmi on his mother's character.

'Who would want to marry Miss Kohla anyway?' Dinsy said.

'I wouldn't mind marrying sixty thousand rupees if it promised to keep its face to the wall when we were in bed,' Shahid said. He was a cynic about women.

People began teasing Dinsy about the smell of talcum powder that emanated from his neat, transformed person.

'What age difference is all right for marriage?' Dinsy asked.

'Ten years younger,' Kishan said authoritatively.

'Older women know more tricks,' Dara said.

'Bepsi wouldn't know any tricks,' Dinsy said. His voice was almost sad.

'It's "Bepsi" now, is it? Not "Miss Kohla"?' I asked.

'Forget it,' was Kolmi's opinion. 'That woman knows the difference between a morsel and a meal.'

When Dinsy was not present, Kolmi would tell us that he doubted whether the old woman had as much money as people said.

Dinsy dropped out of the Chowk crowd. It was known that he spent his evenings with Miss Kohla, accompanying her sometimes to Main Street and carrying her shopping bags.

'She'll soon sack Hukam Ali. He'll get the walking ticket and Dinsy, poor fellow, will be going to buy the dog meat and coriander in the mornings.'

Now Dinsy would only be seen in the Chowk when he came from the New Era classes to buy hot snacks from the bhajia shop, or to get cold drinks from the Kayani to take back to Miss Kohla and her guests.

'You are giving her hot snacks now, are you?' Dara asked.

The Chowk said that Dinsy had gone crazy. He had been seen sitting on chairs with Miss Kohla outside her tiny front door and carrying on earnest conversations with her.

The shorthand and typing examination results didn't come in with the school exams results. They were altogether less spectacular news. On the day they were published, Dinsy came to the Chowk to do a public relations job. He boasted about the number of people who had got through the exam and graduated from the New Era class. For once he too had passed an exam. He bought a round of tea.

'She's teaching you fast fingering, is she?' Shahid asked.

'No non-vegetarian jokes, yaar, I've come to have a cele-bration.'

Mr Mistry also came to the Kayani and boasted that all his girls had got through their exams too.

Dinsy made it known that Mistry was very deficient in shorthand, that he had got his qualifications by post and that he was no good.

It was after that exchange that the war of the typewriting classes began in earnest. Old Mistry was a betting man and one night he struck it rich. Kolmi paid out reluctantly and told the whole Chowk that Mistry had cheated him. He had written the betting slip in what looked to him like shorthand and Kolmi wasn't even certain that Mistry had won. Nevertheless he had paid up.

A few days later news reached the Chowk through Kishan's sister, who was a pupil of old Mistry's, that their class had acquired an 'A S D F G' machine.

'Smugglers again,' Kishan said. 'They never keep their deals. You can buy a British battleship if you're willing to pay them, right here on the pavements of Poona.'

Kishan reported that Mistry had cleaned out his front room and hired some boys to rewire and paint the place. A signwriter was seen on a ladder outside his house. The Post Office had been asked to install a telephone at his business premises. Neon lights followed and metal furniture brought in by truck from Bombay. Plastic chairs, new Japanese electric typewriters, the sky seemed to be the limit.

Kolmi discovered that after cleaning him out, Mistry had moved on to bookies from the City. He had hit every gambling street corner in town and taken all the bookies for a ride. He said he wasn't taking bets from Mistry any more. After a life of losing, the old man must have made thousands of rupees on the cotton figures.

The sign over Mistry's door now said MISTRY'S MODERN CLINIC OF COMMERCE.

'Mistry makes spelling mistakes,' Dinsy said. 'He can't compare or compete.' But the comparison was made by all who saw and the competition was getting hot.

Mistry advertised in the *Poona Messenger* and in a matter of weeks after the renovations he acquired a couple of pupils who came to Dastur Meher Road in cars. The upgraded class of his new clientele attracted more pupils.

Dinsy bought a pot of paint out of his own money and started repainting the sign of the New Era Typing and Shorthand Classes. He fixed the slats of Miss Kohla's wooden gate. He loudly declared that he had urged Miss Kohla to give him a thousand rupees to go to Bombay and fetch new machines for their class, electric typewriters, anything.

A colonel's daughter who had failed her shorthand exams at the New Era transferred to Mistry's classes. Even then, Dinsy told us, Miss Kohla would not part with a single rupee. She didn't understand business. Now she was going to have to fight to keep her livelihood. This bastard Mistry was stealing pupils. How low could a man stoop?

'Anyway, the girl is not even a real colonel's daughter, only a retired colonel's,' he said. He didn't sound as though he drew much consolation from the fact.

More desertions followed. In a few months' time, Old Mistry had bought himself a suit and a little motor scooter and disdained to hang around the Chowk and talk to the likes of Kolmi. His class was thriving.

Dinsy came to Kishan one day with a counter-strategy.

'Your sister Nalini,' he said to Kishan, 'she goes to that man's class, doesn't she?'

'You stick to your Bepsi Kohla and leave my sister alone.'

'No, I don't mean anything bad, yaar. I was just thinking that if she wants to be a good secretary instead of just a typist, she should transfer to New Era. She could learn shorthand from Miss Kohla.'

'She's learning shorthand already,' Kishan replied.

Dinsy laughed. 'From Mistry? She can only learn short-change from that crook.'

'Wake up, yaar,' Kishan said. 'She is learning shorthand. Haven't you ever heard of hired labour?'

'What do you mean?'

'Taking money, doing work? Mistry's got a Goan girl teaching shorthand three days a week now.'

'What?'

'Yes. Miss Kohla's class she was in. Now she teaches for Mistry. Also he's got soft seats. I don't want my sister to get piles.'

Dinsy was crestfallen. It was as though he had been slapped in the face.

'Venus De Cruz? It's that girl, isn't it? Our star pupil a year ago. You see how nobody can be trusted. I keep telling Bepsi to modernize. No electric typewriters, no students.'

Mistry bought plastic folders for all his pupils. In the winter results of the Pitman exam, he got what he called 'cent per cent results' which he advertised in the *Poona Messenger*. Dinsy had been so busy with the war, he had failed his typewriting exams. It was the final straw. He reported that there were only three students enrolled in New Era for the next session. Miss Kohla still wouldn't listen, not to him. If only someone could knock some sense into the stubborn woman's head.

The grass grew taller under the New Era's board. Dinsy's sparkle was gone. One day he came to the Kayani and told us that he had been forbidden entrance to Miss Kohla's house. He could come for one shift of typing classes and then shift off. Hukam Ali reported the truth.

'She has relatives come from Bombay. The business is in a bad way. Nothing can be done. The relatives were shocked to find Dinsy hanging around the house all the time and sent him packing.'

Kishan brought the momentous news to the Chowk. Mistry had announced to his class that he would be closed and they would all get a day off on the occasion of his engagement. He was going to be married.

Invitations reached the more respectable people of the neighbourhood.

My grandfather showed me the one we were sent. It said that Mr Dadabhoy Mistry of Dastur Meher Road was to be married to the niece of Mr and Mrs Adil Chawda of Dadar, Bombay, Miss Bepsi Kohla of Sachapir Street.

The Chowk said the match was good. What else could the poor woman do? It was Hukam Ali who told us that the proposal had come through the Bombay relatives from old Mistry.

'She's not as pathetic as she looks,' Kolmi insisted. 'She must have known there wasn't room enough for two commercial classes in this neighbourhood, so she didn't waste her money on furniture and new machines. That Mistry is a money-hungry old dog.'

Everyone agreed that the New Era and the Modern Clinic would do well to get together.

'It may even stop him making passes at those young Goan girls he hires,' Hukam Ali said.

No one thought of Dinsy. On the day before the wedding he disappeared. The wedding was quite a big affair and Miss Kohla smiled and smiled and smiled. People said old Mistry didn't look fifty years old at all.

When we inquired, Dinsy's father told us that his son was in Bombay and had got himself a good job in a government office doing shorthand and typing.

VI

Confession

Confession D'Souza was one of those boys from the Chowk who wouldn't enter other people's houses. He'd stand at the gate and shout for you. When my grandfather invited him in, he would say, 'No, uncle, call him outside, please.' He was the same age as the other boys of the neighbourhood I hung around with but he was much poorer. He lived in one of the gulleys behind Sachapir Street, the warren of little passages too narrow for more than a bicycle and too slushy and potholed for a smooth ride on one.

Confession was a favourite of the Jesuits who taught him. He only started wearing shoes when he was old enough to go to their school. His mother had five children to bring up without a husband. Confession was the oldest and probably the only one who remembered their father at all, because he'd run away when Confession was six. With another woman, they said on the Chowk, to Bombay to train Alsatians and play the violin in the instant orchestras of the Hindi movies.

'Give your friend your old shoes, you'll get a new pair for New Year, you've got three,' my grandfather said.

I couldn't. I pretended I liked my old pair too much and didn't really want a new pair for New Year. Poverty was embarrassing amongst friends. Besides, I knew that Confession would accept the gift, especially if I took the pair to his house and gave them to him in front of his mother who'd be thankful, but he would resent it. He had huge, accusing and bright black eyes. He was wiry and you could see his ribs under the cotton vests he wore instead of shirts. His cheek was dented with a deep dimple when he smiled.

Shahid told us that when he and Confession first went to the Catholic school together he shared a bench with him and watched Confession frantically rubbing out what he'd copied in one lesson to leave the pages blank for the next one. He used to pretend that the dog-eared and blackened exercise book was new for each subject and was constantly scolded for the state of his one exercise book. It was only when the 'padris', which is what the Jesuits were called, recognized Confession's potential as a scholar and a good Christian, that they gave him a grant for books and clothes and gave his mother money to help bring up the other children.

Throughout our school days, Confession acquired the reputation of being something of a pet of the padris. He was not only the school's star scholar, he was their best footballer, violinist, Confirmation class helper, general dogsbody of the Virgin Mary Mission, and was earmarked by the padris to go to the Jesuit seminary. He was a willing spokesman for the campaigns and propaganda which the padris launched on their pupils.

One such campaign was lectures to the senior boys of the school on the dangers of drink, gambling, and sinning with yourself, 'pulling the wire' or 'playing with your spices' as it was known amongst ourselves.

'For boys of our age, it is not only a mortal sin, Father Coutinho said, it will also turn you mad and then blind.

82

And it gives you funny thoughts, men, like atheism and communism.'

'I heard it gives you dimples first,' Shahid said.

'Kill yourself if you want. God bless you,' Confession replied.

In his final year of school, it was known on the Chowk that Confession had developed an interest in philosophy. He began carrying books with strange titles around with him. They were called *The Critique of Pure Reason* and *Thus Spake Zarathustra*. No one in our circle knew what these books were about, why they had been written or who, apart from Confession, read them. The closest any of our bunch had ever got to philosophy was a book which Kishan had called *How To Win Friends and Influence People*. What we did know was that Confession's books came from the Punjab Book Exchange on Main Street.

We all knew the shop. It was a paying library run by a man called Lajpat. He rented out books at five pice a time, and would buy any book that a client brought in.

I once sold him three books by a poet called Kahlil Gibran, which my uncle had left in our house. Lajpat leafed through them and quoted a price.

'I thought fifty pice each at least,' I said.

'Nobody reads these things, brother,' Lajpat said, making a face. 'If I'm giving you thirty each, it is only for putting in bookcase and giving some show to my shop.'

The 'show' books were in the glass cases and the display window of the Punjab Book Exchange. It was a long narrow shop with a backroom and stairs leading up from it to Lajpat's private residence. The shop itself was divided into two. In the front of the long room were the sorts of books that Confession carried about. The back half was full of shelves and showcases crammed with paperbacks called *Gunsmoke Gold* and *Rust in the Saddle*.

For a reserved section of his customers, there was a third side to the Punjab Book Exchange. Beyond the cowboy trash was the yellow curtain leading to the backroom. Special customers disappeared behind the curtain and came back with brown-paper covered books which had titles like *Strict Schoolmaster's Adventure* and *Report on A Prize-Winning Banana*.

Lajpat was genuinely astonished when Confession went into the shop and asked him to unlock the cases in the front of the shop. No customer had asked for those in three years. The titles weren't even listed in his typed library catalogue. Lajpat would get Confession a book from the cases, but never from the shop window. They were in there, he said, to give respectability to his business; how could he leave gaps and blanks in his respectability?

Regular customers, like Dara and myself, would go straight to the backroom.

Confession carried the books he hired with great pride. 'These books are so tough, they'll scramble up your brain,' he'd say.

One day he was carrying a book which he said even the padris regarded as the hardest book in the world. It had a German title, but had been translated into a strange inaccessible English. It was passed from hand to hand.

'This must be inspired by Hitler,' Kishan said.

'It's not politics, it's theology,' Confession replied, with his voice conveying his contempt in spite of the smile he flashed. 'It's fakeology,' Ashish said, grabbing the book and throwing it like a discus.

Confession ran to pick it up. 'It's Lajpat's book, you fool. It costs me ten pice for reading and fifty pice for deposit. No good talking intellectual things with you all.'

When Confession left, Shahid told us that he was carrying around the hardest book in the world because a bigwig from the Jesuit seminary was going to visit their school, the following day. 'He's always showing off with the padris, yaar, giving impression.'

On the day of this important visit, St Vincent's was playing the town's Parsi school in the football league finals. It was in the field behind Vincent's and a bit of a town event to which all the regulars on the Chowk went.

The spectators gathered in the hot afternoon. I raced home from school and went with Dara and Kishan to the match. The Parsi team arrived by bicycle with their coach. They changed in a corner of the field into their gear. The Vincent's team, being on home ground, scattered itself amongst the spectators till the whistle called them to assemble around the young padri who was refereeing the game. Confession knew that a lot of eyes were on him. He went to the goalposts and proceeded to change his clothes in full view of the public. The Vincent's team was in shorts and yellow and green tee-shirts. The players had left little piles of their school uniforms and bags and books all along the borders of the field.

The St Vincent's team always played football without boots. They taped their feet in thin bandages and galloped about lifting their knees to get into the spirit of the game. Confession led them into battle. The crowd cheered.

As the game began, a few of the padris left the crowd and ventured to the edge of the field, shouting encouragement to their players and parading their privileged position. The bigwig from the seminary stood with a couple of young padris behind the Vincent's goalpost, with folded arms, watching the game and smiling benignly. He had been told by the padris about Confession and their ambition to initiate him to the brotherhood. That afternoon he had heard him play the violin in the school hall. Now he would watch him captain the team to victory.

The game started badly for Vincent's. The Parsi team scored an easy goal. Confession was all over the field. He was playing centre forward but threw himself enthusiastically into defence and began shouting at his team as they missed passes and kicked the ball straight to their opponents.

'Come on, Vincent's,' the seminary bigwig shouted.

The score at half-time was still the same. St Vincent's were losing a record they had held ever since the league began. The tension amongst the spectators was mounting. Confession gathered his team and went into a huddle with them. They came out of it only when the whistle blew. A new strategy was abroad.

The strategy seemed to pay off and Vincent's scored a goal. Then they went on to a fast bid for victory, keeping the ball constantly in their scoring half and holding five of their best defenders like a stone wall at the half line. Confession and the two forwards were going to manage the attack.

My eyes were on the game till Shahid nudged me.

'Look, look, Confession's left his fat books on his clothes to impress the baldy.'

The padris at the goalpost must have said something to the seminary chief about Confession, because one of them bent down and picked up the book that Confession had left lying on top of his discarded clothes. The seminary chief leafed through the book.

Then something very strange happened. Confession glanced down the field and saw one of the padris rummaging in his pile of clothing and going through his school bag, presumably to find more books to impress the big chief.

Confession missed a pass and the crowd roared. He was running down the field towards the half line. It seemed a crazy move. Three stalwarts of the opposing team ran towards him. Confession was sprinting past his own team's backs. We saw him run the length of the field and snatch his school bag from the padri's hand. He was shouting something that we didn't catch. The game had stopped. The players and the spectators were watching this display beyond the goalposts. The padri held on to Confession's satchel and Confession pulled at it. The goalkeeper joined in on the padri's side. There was a surge of spectators towards the goalposts now. The referee blew a frantic whistle, like a policeman dealing with berserk traffic.

Within a few seconds, Confession and the padri were on the ground, wrestling each other. Other padris joined in and pulled Confession, who was swearing like he had never done before, off the brother. It was his private property, he said, his private possessions.

'You bloody padris don't own me. You want to search everything, look into your mother's knickers because you think you pay for the fees.' It took three boys and two Jesuits to hold Confession, still swearing and kicking, on the ground. The satchel's contents were being rifled by the deputy head. Out of it emerged the brown paper-covered books. The deputy head's eyes bulged as he scrutinized them. He was in a rage.

'Confession,' he said, intoning the syllables in his nose, 'put on your clothes, dear boy, and go home.'

The game was called off. Confession arose from the huddle, no longer struggling. His big black eyes were full of tears and his eyelashes glistened with the moisture. He went home. The crowd broke. The padris and the big bald chief retreated to the parlours on the upper floors of the school buildings.

Shahid reported events the next day. 'Very bad for him, no good. Father Costello found six books from Lajpat's in his bag, all with blue stamps on brown cover.'

'My father won't like it. He sent me to Lajpat for some Zane Grey cowboy books, but Lajpat has shut for a few days,' Dara said. 'Poor Lajpat, the padris are trying to ruin his business. The dogs sent the police and two padris went there themselves. Lajpat showed them his register and they took down all the names of the filth that Confession has been hiring for two years now. Poor fellow.'

'He took *The Nun's Delight* three times last month. Not a bad book,' Shahid said.

'Lajpat has taken all his good stock upstairs. Police can't touch what a man has in his bedroom but he might give up the business, he said. He's buying a printing press second-hand from the City and starting new business,' Dara added.

For a week Confession didn't go to school. His mother knew that her son was in disgrace but didn't know why until a padri was sent to the household to negotiate his repentance and re-entry into the school. His penance was standing on the school stage at assembly, like a man in the stocks. The padris had told him that he had to lead the school's prayers on resisting temptation and asking the Virgin's grace. He was removed from the boy-scout troop and from the football team. Some expected a tear of contrition from Confession when these sentences were pronounced, but his eyes remained shifty and dry.

Four months after his public disgrace, three months before the final school exam, the quiet paved quadrangle of St Vincent's was showered with a fall of badly printed leaflets from a third floor window. They were called *St Vincent's Chooth,* the cunt of St Vincent. The leaflet was written in perfect English. Each of the items on it accused the Jesuits of some dirt. One said that Father Angelo took boys up to his room after violin lessons and gave them bread and jam. Why was this bread and jam handed out to defenceless youngsters? The item said that an innocent third standard boy had emerged from the holy father's room rubbing his backside. The other items talked of sports between the nuns and the Jesuits and the third one accused a well-respected Father of being a bigamist before he took his vows.

There was a riot in the playground. The *Chooth* threatened worse scandals to come. The padris went mad. They rushed about the quadrangle gathering every scrap of paper from every boy they accosted. Classes were suspended and a steady stream of boys was called in for inquisitions about who had been seen doing what in which part of the school.

When Confession was finally cornered, he refused to confess. He stuck stubbornly to his denial of any knowledge of the leaflets or the scandals they mentioned. A bible was fetched and he swore on it. The Head was convinced that the language and phrases used were the work of one of the more academic seniors. The police traced the leaflets to Lajpat's printing press.

Just three months before his final exam, Confession was expelled from the school. He became something of a hero in our neighbourhood. He became the most deadly enemy that the padris and Christianity had known in our part of the world. He announced that he had embraced the Hindu religion and that he had changed his name to Prabhat because he didn't want the slur of a Christian name. On weekdays we saw him studying on the benches on Master Paranjpe's verandah. He was going to do his exams as an external student.

On the night the results were declared he sat up with us on the steps of the Kayani awaiting them. His name was in the headline of the paper which published them. He was first of all the candidates who had sat the exams. His mother, who had been weeping and praying and not understanding for three months, came out to the Chowk and kissed him in front of us. Apart from his overall first class first, the examiners also announced that Prabhat D'Souza had won the prize for English and for Religious Education.

'The virgin Mary has answered all my prayers,' his mother said. 'The Fathers will be so pleased, so happy.'

Dara, Kishan, Shahid, Ashish and I also passed our matric that night. In the months which followed, we joined college and Confession went to work.

By the time I joined the staff of the *Poona Messenger* as a part-time reporter, Confession D'Souza, now known as Prabhat, was assistant editor. The *Messenger* was a relatively new paper in our town and each year it hired students from the colleges to do reporting, sub-editing, running around for advertisements and other jobs that it didn't want to pay unionized reporters to do. We, the amateurs, were paid by the column-inch and had to do a few hours of desk work for the privilege of being media men. Prabhat would mercilessly cut our stories to the bare bone in order to save the *Messenger*'s money and leave space for himself to write features in the daily four-page sheet.

As a writer he had a reputation all round town. He worked tirelessly, wrote two-and-a-half to three of the sheets each day, proofread the whole shambles each night before sending it down to the men on the ground floor who typeset and printed the whole thing on primitive machines. Prabhat wrote most of the editorials and ran what he called 'campaigns' in the newspaper; on the cleanliness of butchers' knives in the meat-market, on paving the gulleys behind Sachapir Street where he still lived with his mother and brothers and sisters, on what he called the 'rackets' which missionaries used to recruit the poor to the ways of the cross.

Prabhat would drop in at the Kayani on his way to work in the mornings and sip a double char and pick up the gossip and hints of scandal that floated about like cigarette smoke in that atmosphere. He would pass on fascinating information about local worthies to his old friends on the Chowk, stuff that was 'not for publication in our lifetime', or stories that were 'protected by black money'.

The year I began work for the *Messenger,* a girl called Zeenat who was in college with me was also taken on as a part-timer. After a few weeks I noticed that this girl Zeenat was always being given desk jobs by Prabhat and I was always sent out on my bicycle on outside assignments. I knew Zeenat somewhat. She was reputed to be one of the richest girls in college. She was certainly one of the prettiest in a perky sort of way. She was thin and tall, always wore a salwar kamiz, did her hair in two tight pigtails and arranged a stray lock on her forehead as a mark of modernity. She was driven to college in a car by a chauffeur or by one of her elder brothers. She came to the dingy offices of the *Messenger* in the same style. When her work at the office was over she'd be picked up by car and taken home, sitting in the backseat, looking regally out of the window. I never considered her much of an asset to the *Messenger* as she could hardly ever get away from the watchful eye of her brothers or the routine that the chauffeur-driven car pinned her to.

The workers at the *Messenger* knew what Prabhat was up to with Zeenat. He would stay in the office when he gave her desk work to do and take twice the time he normally took over proofreading the galleys. Then he started to take her, for snatched half-hours, to the Chinese restaurant further down the road from the newspaper offices. It was said that they went into the private booths reserved by the restaurant for families.

Prabhat soon took to appearing at the gates of the college in the day time on the scooter that the newspaper had bought him. Zeenat would skip lectures and take off on the pillion of the Vespa and come back just in time for her car to pick her up.

Their love affair was a secret only from her family. Everyone else knew about it and gossiped about spotting the pair in Empress Gardens or in a remote cafe of the City. In the office they kept their distance. Only their eyes told the story. The editor of the *Messenger,* Mr Able Patrick, talked to Prabhat a few times and tried to caution him.

'Arey, watch what you're doing, yaar,' Mr Patrick said. 'You act as though you don't know who this girl is. You know her father has so much influence in Poona, he can order a total eclipse of the sun. You are a Christian boy, she is a Muslim girl from a good family, this can't go on. And what about the paper and the danger to me?'

'I'm not Christian, Patrick sahib, I told you I am Hindu and that is what I shall remain unless Zeenat wants me to change, herself. But she won't. Are we living in a modern India or is it still filled with all this caste and religious nonsense and headache? This paper is for free love,' Prabhat said. His tone was defiant, but he sat and fiddled with his pen and only glanced up now and then.

'This paper is for staying in business,' Able Patrick said, 'but don't take it wrong. You're like my son, I'm just giving one advice.'

The 'one advice' obviously didn't penetrate, because Prabhat fearlessly took up a story that was causing a stir in our neighbourhood and wrote an editorial on it. The story concerned a boy and girl whom Prabhat and the rest of us on the Chowk knew. It caused ructions in our neighbourhood. Akbar, a Muslim boy from our street ran away with a Parsi girl called Shireen from the Parsi colony in Synagogue Street. The boy's parents brought the couple back from Bombay and attempted to talk to her parents who had declared to everyone that their daughter Shireen had been disowned by them, but they'd still get her back and teach her the price of racial disloyalty.

Akbar's parents had the difficult task of persuading Shireen's father and mother and advisors that they ought to be allowed to marry, because they would only run away again and, besides, Shireen was pregnant. They agreed, reluctantly and after two weeks of melodrama. The arrangement was the talk of the town.

Some said there'd be religious riots. The more bigoted Parsis, including Mr Minocher Toot, formed a posse and went and stood with black flags outside Akbar's house, to which the registrar had been called for the wedding. One of Akbar's younger brothers emerged from the house with his friends and beat up the black-flag-wallahs. The police were called.

Out of our gang Ashish was Akbar's special friend. He knew about the couple's plans before they eloped. We knew that he had pawned his gold watch and given Akbar the money. We supported Ashish and Akbar and Shireen. We were children of a new age but didn't feel confident enough to challenge the filthy gossip and prejudice that emerged on the Chowk as a result of the whole business.

'If I was her father, I'd kill her rather than let a Muslim touch her,' Kolmi said, his Adam's apple jumping in indignation.

'This brat Shireen must think there's something wrong with Parsi manhood,' Samson said, adjusting his elephantine bottom on the wooden chair and scratching his balls.

We remained silent. Prabhat responded.

The editorial of the *Messenger* called on readers to support 'mixed marriages', to emerge from the dark medievalism of their prejudices and from religious fanaticism. It quoted Gandhi. It quoted Nehru. It reminded people that this was 1962. 'The young are determined to be people and citizens, not of ghettoes and religions, but of free India. What does this freedom mean? Does it not mean the right to marry whom you chose? The right to spend your life as a constructive citizen with another citizen of your choice? One generation won freedom for India, another generation is teaching them the ways of freedom.'

It was a brave editorial. It didn't win Confession the hearts and minds of the neighbourhood. He had signed it and knew that when he walked into the Kayani again he would be given the cold shoulder or rank abuse.

'Here comes the champion of illegitimate half-castes,' Samson said. The editorial had been discussed to shreds that day.

'What can you expect from a Christian who has turned himself into an untouchable Hindu?' Kolmi said.

'Listen,' Prabhat responded, raising his voice. 'Listen to me you stupid sons of fertile women. If this neighbourhood, where I was born and have lived, doesn't shut the filthy mouths that infest it like a disease, I will publish in that newspaper the name of every man who has slept with servant girls, every man whose face has broken out like rotten tomatoes in diseases picked up from prostitutes. Did they enquire about the religion of the prostitute before they paid her their bookie's wages? You hypocrites, you sons of bitches. Be sure to buy the paper tomorrow and get your wives to read it. We'll see who wants to really stand up for their mumbo jumbo.'

The cafe was silenced. Prabhat came and sat at our table and sipped his tea. We were full of admiration for the courage which had emboldened him to speak, though we knew that it was not simply his conviction; it was a gesture of his love for Zeenat.

It was a difficult love. Once when I was working late at the office, Zeenat's brother arrived to pick her up. He'd delivered her there some hours before. He looked as though he was about to tear the place up when Able Patrick told him that Zeenat was out interviewing some women. The rest of us in the office pretended to be very busy, our noses in raw print. We knew it was a lie.

'When is she coming back. She said eight o'clock? You keep girls out till this time, Mr Patrick?' The brother was adamant. He was offered a chair and sat by the door, looking at his watch.

'You know how women are,' Able Patrick said. 'You mustn't be worried, Mr Khan, she will talk and talk with the Poona Club librarian. Their library was completely burnt up last week and we have sent Miss Khan, together with some experienced journalists of course, to see what they are doing about new stock and etcetera.'

I could see from the way the brother twirled his moustaches, that he didn't believe a word of it. When Prabhat's Vespa growled to a halt downstairs, he leapt out of his chair, and without saying a word to Able Patrick, disappeared down the stairs. We heard his voice and Zeenat's voice and the clack of two car doors. Prabhat came up looking guilty. He didn't say a word. He snatched the proofs from my hand and picked up his blue pencil.

The next day we heard that Zeenat's services had been withdrawn from the *Messenger*. She didn't come to college and the rumour spread that her father had beaten her up and then called the doctor to attend to her wounds. At the office Prabhat moved about from print shop to editor's desk in gloom. For days after that he didn't come to the cafes at the Chowk and spent half his night at the office, telling everyone that he was fed up with the misprints in the paper and he would personally fire all the typesetters if they didn't stop coming to the job with drink and ganja oozing out of their eyeballs.

The only remark he made to me was after he sent me to investigate a story about the murder of five 'untouchables', landless peasants, in a village near Poona. I was conscious of the honour bestowed. Normally it would have been his story and he would have pursued it with the seriousness he was admired for.

'The landlords are guilty as Judas,' he said to me. 'Write it so that the reader understands that. You know, Farrukh, the rich can do what they fucking like in our country. Free press? What press, men, they can press you into the wet ground, like we press earthworms in the monsoon.'

He was right. I had to go to the police for the details of the story. The villagers I spoke to for two days, wandering with my pen and pad around the district, refused to say anything. The police superintendent told me that he was going to arrest one of the landlords. They had evidence. Prabhat took my facts and listened to my opinion and wrote a brilliant editorial to supplement what I had written.

I sat with him after the editor and the rest of the staff had gone home. He leafed through files of statistics and research documents. The editorial said that landlordism was responsible for the murders. It talked about the system of enforced poverty under which the victims of the murders lived and of the caste divisions and the unequal justice of the police force that was investigating the murders. He held me by the wrist as I was leaving.

'I'll give you contact in the local police force, you follow this up. Just now I'm not feeling like going out too much.'

The murders weren't solved. Prabhat was furious, first with me, then with the police, and then with the sheet of paper on which he was writing. The editorial the next day attacked the police. He accused them of siding with murderers. He accused them of taking bribes from landlords and being blind to the principles of a civilized society. Strong stuff, stronger than the *Messenger* had ever printed. It even won some approval on the Chowk. In the Chowk anything that was anti-police was bound to win approval.

'An editor who tells the truth about the "hungries" must be all right,' Kolmi said. A few days after the editorial, Prabhat appeared unexpectedly on the Chowk. Shahid came into the Kayani and informed us that he was getting steadily drunk at Uncle Frankie's joint. Ashish and Dara were with me and we decided to go and talk to him. As we got to

Uncle Frankie's, Prabhat staggered out and climbed on to his Vespa.

'We've come to talk to you,' I said.

'I've got an important editorial to write,' he said and the Vespa went into first gear and lurched into the darkness of the gulley, now paved for such traffic.

It was a vicious editorial. It attacked the morals and the position of middle-class girls.

'These young women, no better than the prostitutes who sell themselves to the highest bidder, are wasting the resources of our poor country. They crowd our colleges, they insist on an education. All for what? To give themselves to prospective husbands for smaller dowries. They are a generation adrift, content to move under the direction of their fathers who own industry and usurp the high offices in our so-called democracy. . .'

When I got to the *Messenger* office that evening after college, Prabhat wasn't there. The editor was holding his head in his hands, his elbows on his desk. Prabhat had been dismissed, he told me.

'He is an idiot, such an idiot, men, what could I do? They all came to me, the owner and three other fellows, businessmen. Prabhat doesn't understand these things. They were after his blood, men, I sent him home.'

'Didn't you read the editorial before it went down?' I asked. 'I always trust him not to bring his personal business into this paper. Such a brilliant boy. Anyway, don't worry, I'll calm these people down and bring him back. Tomorrow if I can. All he has to do is apologize to them personally.'

I went down to the ground floor, to the print shop.

'What happened here?' I asked the chief typesetter.

'Arrey, don't ask,' he said, 'her father came and two

brothers. They brought some rich and very influential people with them and told Patrick that Prabhat has to be dismissed for writing filthy things.'

'What?'

'That's not all. She was here. Zeenat came, driving the car herself very late last night, and was talking to Prabhat. She told him that her father and brother were going to marry her off to a rich Muslim from Ahmedabad who owned the only air-conditioning machine factory in India. Prabhat was crying, she was crying, and then the brothers come and beat him up. They beat him so badly that Patrick had to take him home in rickshaw. See the scooter still there.'

Zeenat's approaching wedding was big news in college too. The news of the fight between her brothers and Prabhat had also reached the campus.

On the Chowk it was known that Prabhat had forfeited his Vespa. He was hiring a bicycle from Ahura cycle mart to get about. I heard that he'd offered his services to the *Messenger's* rival, the *Poona Daily News* and had been turned down. He had even gone to Minocher Toot and proposed to him that the *Synagogue Spotlight* could be improved by hiring him.

Prabhat was in a state when we saw him. He spent all his time in Uncle Frankie's, drinking. On one occasion when we joined him there, his mother came to the tavern and begged him to go home with her. His little sister was very ill, she said. Prabhat waved his glass of cashew liquor at her.

'This is no place for a lady. My father married you for love. You are no whore. You weren't sold to the highest bidder. This is no place for a lady. Get out.'

'Your sister is very ill,' Mrs D'Souza said.

'You need a doctor, woman, not an unemployed journalist,' Prabhat said.

Dara took her out of the tavern. Shahid went with her to her house. They assured her that we'd get Prabhat back as soon as possible. It was best to leave him alone.

'The *Times Of India* has offered me a job in Bombay,' Prabhat said, 'I could go to fucking America and work for *Newsweek* if I wanted.'

Shahid said that Mrs D'Souza was crying as he and Dara accompanied her home.

'God preserve us from the cleverness of our children,' was what she said. 'If he hadn't been so clever he would have been earning some bread for his brothers and sisters. I don't care about myself. All he thinks about is this Muslim girl.'

'I defied the masturbating Jesuits,' Prabhat said, leaning on my shoulder as I took him home. 'I exposed the smugglers. Look at this stone which we are walking on, Farrukh. You think this stone would have come to this gulley without me calling and campaigning for improved pavementation? Who do these business wallahs think they are? They have daughters? Everybody has daughters!'

Three days after that Zeenat was married to the air-conditioning magnate from Ahmedabad. The night before the wedding her brothers came to the Chowk in two cars and asked for Prabhat D'Souza's address.

'I'll give Prabhat one day's takings on the cotton figures if he runs off with this girl before she gets married,' Kolmi said. He had obviously changed his mind on mixed marriages; or maybe it was just that in this one no Parsis were involved. We heard that Zeenat was married in style at her suburban house. The Governor of the State was the chief guest and arrived in his ensigned car, with a motorcycle escort.

On the day of the wedding there were no editions of the *Messenger*. I went to the offices and was faced with a padlock on the door. That was mysterious.

The day after the wedding the paper hit the streets with a big black sash printed diagonally across the front page. The lead story said ASSISTANT EDITOR OF MESSENGER MURDERED.

Full of the achievements of Prabhat D'Souza, stained with the sentiments of Able Patrick, the story said that the assistant editor of the *Messenger* had been found murdered, his head beaten in with a blunt instrument in Empress Gardens. Next to his body, in the bushes, were a couple of hired bicycles, one gent's bike, one lady's. The article didn't mention Zeenat or speculate about who had a motive for murdering him, but it was said on the Chowk that Zeenat had disappeared on the evening before her wedding and the owner of the cycle mart said that he would give evidence, if the family allowed the case to come to trial, about who had hired bicycles from him. Because Prabhat was a boy from our neighbourhood, several people on the Chowk vowed to find out which thugs had been imported to find Zeenat and deal with Prabhat on that last night of recklessness. The case never came to trial. The police said there was no evidence. The owners sacked Able Patrick the editor, for 'speculating' about murder and 'interfering with justice'.

At Prabhat's funeral, which jammed the D'Souza gulley and overflowed into Sachapir Street, his mother broke down and cried, throwing herself on the coffin. The padris from St Vincent's turned out in force and Father Angelo pulled Mrs D'Souza off the coffin and helped to silence the howling children.

VII

Chamak

The Naz cafe on the corner of Main Street, opposite the West End cinema, was an altogether grander place than either the Kayani or the Sachapir restaurants of the Chowk. It had glass tables and a garden and terrace. If you sat in the garden in the dry seasons, or on the covered terrace, you had to buy a double char. The poor stayed downstairs. College boys hung around there all evening, showing off their clothes by parading Main Street and returning periodically to the Naz which was used as a meeting place and a low-grade bistro. It had a juke box and the reputation for being the fastest place in town.

The boss crowd of the Naz cafe in the days when my friends and I walked Main Street was a trio of bad hats called Avtar Singh, Harish and Chamak. Chamak was a gangling youth with a big nose crowned with a perpetual pimple which he wore like a trinket of jewellery. He polished his pimple and made it shine. He had curly hair which stuck out fiercely from the sides of his head and he always wore startling clothes: red and green bush shirts with luminous ties painted with Mickey Mouse and nude girls and palm trees.

Chamak was recognized as the brains behind the activities of the trio. Harish was a muscle man, veteran of a hundred fights. He had a reputation for bodily lifting his opponents and throwing them a distance – over railway bridges, into trees, into the monsoon puddles which left them wet and ridiculous.

Avtar Singh always wore a white turban. He knew muscle men who worked for his father's truck garage in the City and had a brother who owned a farm in a village a few miles from Poona.

Chamak was ambitious. In our second year of college he stood for the elected post of Joint General Secretary, or JGS. The JGS was the head of the student body, the only elected post in college. His or her job was to organize a 'social' at the end of each academic year and there was some power and money attached to the position, because this 'social' lasted a week with sports and dances and music recitals and competitions of all sorts. The JGS was given a budget by the college to pay bands and contractors. It was common knowledge that the Joint General Secretary got rich by taking a cut from the contractors and fiddling the bills and amounts of money that were doled out to the drama troupes and artists of the college.

A rule of the college was that no money was to be spent on the election, but this rule was always ignored. The candidates would print handbills and swear honesty and their supporters would stage stunts to attract crowds together and speeches would be made from the floor of the canteen and from the steps of the Arts Block.

'If you elect me, I swear to ban Russi Dinshaw and his Spare Parts.'

(*Cheers.*)

'Last year, after they played only Hindi tunes, I threw the saxophonist personally into the hedge.'

(*More cheers.*)

'If you elect the same gang again, you will only get tea and bananas like last year. How many people got food poisoning from the sweets?'

(*Various answers.*)

'I have a surprise for the electors. Elvis Presley is visiting Bombay and my uncle is managing his tour. He will definitely be asked to come and play at the dance.'

(*Jeers.*)

The lectures and tutorials would grind to a halt over the election period and the Principal would send the unofficial police force of the college, the khaki-clad peons who kept order in the classes and corridors, to confiscate all handbills on sight.

Chamak began electioneering early that year. The college was divided into social crowds and Chamak went around buttering up the supposed leaders of each crowd by complimenting them on their clothes or on the size of their muscles. He even lent out his portable tape-recorder to people for a week at a time. He borrowed Kishan's book called *Popular Jokes For All Occasions* and by-hearted several of the best. When election week came round, he changed his strategy.

The change came as something of a shock to the rest of the college. His tactics may not have been dictated by his renowned cunning alone; they were probably governed by nobler motives. Chamak was in love.

The girl he was in love with was called Sushila. She was large and sturdy with a dark-green birthmark the size of a rupee on her cheek. Chamak said he thought she had lovely dimples, they bloomed when she smiled. Sushila never smiled. She was very stern and was known to us as 'Jhansi-ki-Rani'.

She'd won the title by being the Regimental Sergeant Major of the Women's Battalion of the National Cadet Corps. Twice a week the girls of the college would parade in their khaki uniforms, carrying rifles and sten-guns and even learning to drive tanks. Jhansi wore an impeccably starched and stiff uniform, carried a swagger stick and tucked her hair, scraped back in a tight bun, into her khaki beret.

She didn't speak to boys. The only time I heard her speak was when she was shouting commands to her troops. She had a reputation for not being able to take a joke. Once when some rascal made a dirty crack about her swagger stick, she walked up to him in the canteen and slapped him across the face. It caused a sensation. The rascal was about to slap her back, but Harish intervened, shouting 'Jhansi, keep cool', before dragging the joker by the collar and throwing him into the hedge outside the Chemistry block.

Jhansi didn't thank Harish. 'Don't call me stupid names,' she said and walked away.

In election week, after his candidacy had been announced, Chamak was sitting with Harish and Avtar in the canteen discussing strategy. At four o'clock he detached himself and walked over to the sports pavilion behind the playing fields. The Women's Battalion of the NCC came marching past and Chamak started shouting out commands to them. Some of the girls giggled and the more disciplined only smiled, their stiff arms and proud chests betrayed by their amusement. Chamak kept up a constant barrage of commands.

Jhansi was standing in the centre of the field and she saw some of her girls turn their heads towards Chamak who had squatted like a crow on the top tier of the pavilion. She called the parade to a halt and ran up to face the troops. She addressed them and said that their marching was disgraceful.

'Oh ho ho, Napoleon is angry,' Chamak said, cupping his hands to his mouth.

Jhansi ignored him. She got her troops to turn left and commence marching.

'Goodbye, my legionnaires. Farewell, France,' Chamak intoned, in a voice full of faded sorrow. The history students amongst the girls giggled.

After the parade Jhansi saluted the officer in charge and the army trucks which brought the rifles and the regular army personnel drove off. The girls dispersed. Jhansi dusted her khaki trousers and made her stiff way to the bicycle stands. Chamak was already there. She walked past him as though he was part of the hedge. She got her bicycle and wheeled it to the gate. From the canteen doorway we watched Chamak barring her path. Avtar whistled, two fingers in his mouth.

To our surprise, Jhansi was talking to Chamak. For a full five minutes they conversed, her bicycle between them. Chamak was gesticulating. Harish even said that he saw her smile.

'You should be worried about the election, not "chancing" with Jhansi,' Avtar said when Chamak returned.

'I was, yaar, I was.'

'Was what?'

'Look, her father is a big man in politics, yaar. He was disqualified last year for using too many jeeps in his campaign. I told her I found it out.'

'You are trying to blackmail her?'

'Listen, cloth-head,' Chamak said, alluding to Avtar's turban, 'I don't know why you can't even think when the sun goes down and it becomes cool under your turban. How many women are there in the college? Who is the leader of them all?'

'I don't know,' Avtar said. It was a new idea.

'I was talking to Sushila. . .'

'Jhansi?'

'I said Sushila.'

'She'll never vote for you. She thinks you're an immoral loafer.'

'I am, but I can change. What she said was that she is not interested in who wins the election because it's a rascals' feast, not for girls. Not safe. Her father won't let her go.'

'So forget it then.'

'No, you fool. Suppose you were a girl and your father or somebody wouldn't let you come to a rascal's feast. Then suppose the whole social was changed. Decent poetry readings, music recitals, not all this dhingana. Father would send you. No kissing in public, lots of lady teachers, all safe.'

'You were telling dirty jokes over the microphone last year,' Harish objected.

'That was last year. If this kind of thing goes on, there won't be even one girl pupil left in Wadia College.'

'So you've become a saint after two minutes' talk with Jhansi?'

'You drink too much snake-juice liquor,' Chamak said to Harish. 'If there are six hundred and seventy-five girls who will vote for a saint, then the saint wins.'

Avtar was despondent. That morning he had had a thousand handbills printed with a cartoon of Chamak's nose and pimple. The handbills promised hilarious entertainment and a special election day treat.

'All right. We've got to change our tactics now,' Chamak said. 'Tell your brother that we don't need the carts and the dancers. We don't want to drive the decent people away.'

They had planned to get two bullock carts from Avtar's brother's farm and to load them with supporters dressed as eunuchs. Chamak had planned to wear a sari and a wig himself and dance in public to beg votes.

'I've already told my brother,' Avtar said.

'You're brother's not as stupid as you. Just tell him you've changed your mind. I want to win this thing, yaar.'

'Don't be silly,' Harish interjected. 'These stupid decent girls don't even come to college on voting day. I've already hired some drumwallahs and harmonium players.'

'I'll make sure the decent people come. No drums, no harmoniums.'

'You're just "chancing" Jhansi,' Avtar said.

Chamak was serious. The next day he turned up in college wearing a plain white kurta, over tight cotton pyjamas. He announced that he wasn't going to hang around the canteen any more, he was going to attend all his lectures. We heard that he stood up in the history lecture before the tutor arrived and asked for the votes of the 'decent' people in college. He said that he was going to start a campaign to clean up college and that the students ought to be proud of the place of learning where they were privileged to be.

The next day he issued a leaflet asking for votes. It said, 'Chamak Punwani will see that the annual social is a decent affair, without all the immorality that it has seen in the past. At the dance people should come decently dressed and be proud of their Indian heritage. No more can-can skirts and low-cut dresses. All Marathi and Hindi Music. No non-vegetarian dishes at the big dinner. No kissing and dancing in Western style. . .'

He distributed the leaflet himself in the morning, but by the afternoon a squad of girls had joined him. Jhansi herself gave me one of his leaflets.

'What shall we do? He's gone crazy,' Avtar said, 'He's all alone now, on his own,' Harish said.

I wanted to say he wasn't, but I kept quiet. Chamak had touched a political vein, I felt, which would lead him to a mine of resentment against the 'western' ways of the crowd that dominated our college, with their noise and tomfoolery.

People stopped Chamak in the corridors and argued with him.

'I am not simply trying to win votes. It is very high time that this college became Indianized and moral.'

When Chamak came into the canteen, Avtar called to him. Chamak didn't even turn his head to acknowledge the greeting. He walked straight up to a table at which Jhansi was sitting with five other girls. We saw him lean across the table and smile at her and begin a conversation. Then he drew up a chair and sat down. Avtar stormed out of the canteen like a jealous lover who'd been slighted. Jhansi saw him go. She looked at the door and smiled and her dimples showed.

The day before polling day Chamak issued a second leaflet. This one had a complete programme for cleaning up Wadia College. It went so far as to say that lecturers should wear national dress when they stood in front of a class, and if the principal was to retain his standing as a published philosopher he should write some Hindu philosophy and not all this western stuff he was producing in his textbooks.

Chamak was going to win the election. His opponents had tried speaking against his campaign. One of them perpetrated the theory that Cliff Richard had been born in Poona and was on the verge of returning, but the spirit had gone out of the opposing campaigns. Avtar and Harish sat listlessly in the canteen.

'The bloody old dog has learnt some new tricks,' Harish said.

'Five years I have brought him up and trained him. For what, for these people, for Jhansi-ki-rani?' said Avtar.

Jhansi and a group of girls came into the canteen and sat at the furthest table they could find from Harish and Avtar.

'I'm going to buy a new Lambretta with the money after Chamak wins,' Avtar said, raising his voice so that they could hear.

Harish caught on.

'First he'll have to pay all the liquor bills he's run up at Uncle Frankie's. If our boy doesn't win this, he'll be finished. Only way to get the kind of money he needs, yaar.'

Jhansi and the other girls must have heard the remarks, but they ignored them. Chamak came into the canteen, his hands full of election bills. He spotted Avtar and Harish and went over to their table.

'It looks like we're going to win,' Avtar said.

'Look, no hard feelings, I wish you the best of luck tomorrow,' Harish said. 'I just want to talk to you one second. Will you step outside with me?' Harish put his arm around Chamak's shoulder. Jhansi and her girls saw them go out together. Avtar paid the bill and raising his thumb towards the girls shouted, 'Now that we are together, nobody else stands a chance. Vote for Chamak Punwani,' and left the canteen.

Chamak told his followers that on election day itself he was going to abide strictly by the Principal's rules. He wasn't going to do any more on the actual day than address a rally from the steps of the sports pavilion.

It was the right decision. Two hundred people, mostly girls, gathered to listen to Chamak's speech. All around college the other election bandwagons were rolling. One or two candidates had done the best they could by bringing drummers and trumpeters who marched around the college compound.

Chamak mounted the steps of the pavilion after a few words with Jhansi and clapped his hands to attract everybody's attention. He began to speak. He started by saying that most students of the college came there and paid their fees to study, pass their exams and get good jobs. There were others who came there to gamble and fool about and train themselves as playboys. They disregarded all Indian traditions and treated the college like a love camp, running after girls and trying to win cheap popularity. He knew that some changes had to be made here and now and throughout his campaign he had said so loudly and clearly.

'Some people are saying that I am against all fun. How can anyone be against good clean entertainment? If I am elected I am going to be a servant of all the people in the college. My feeling today, after seeing all of you gathered here to listen to me, is that we are all going to win together. I have always been a friend of fun-loving people. They will vote for me too.'

Chamak was sweating with enthusiasm and he kept acknowledging with smiles and modest waves of his hand the occasional clap he got from the girls around Jhansi.

Before he finished his speech a commotion began at the gates of the college. There was the sound of drums and horns and shouting. Heads were turned in the crowd. A procession came round the corner of the Arts block. Two bullock carts loaded with brightly-clad figures, followed by hundreds of clapping and dancing students, lumbered towards the pavilion. Chamak stopped speaking. His whole audience had now turned round to see what was going on.

On the side of both carts were huge painted signs saying VOTE FOR CHAMAK PUNWANI — THE ONLY MAN WHO CAN SUPPLY MORE GIRLS FOR THE SOCIAL. Holding the reins of one of the bullocks, standing in the front of the cart was Avtar Singh. He wasn't wearing a turban. He had let his long hair loose and he was wearing a red sar and a gold blouse. He was grotesquely made up with lipstick and rouge. His square jaw protruded out of this mask of paint. He had stuffed the blouse to give the impression of enormous breasts and as the cart moved, he wiggled his hips to the beat of the drum and harmonium playing behind him. In the cart which followed was Harish. He was wearing shorts and a purple bra and nothing else and he too was dancing with his arms above his head and his hairy armpits showing.

Avtar started a 'VOTE FOR CHAMAK' slogan as the carts drew closer and the crowd around him took it up.

'They're drunk. Ignore them. They've come to spoil my campaign. I know Avtar Singh, just leave them,' Chamak shouted, shrieking above the din of the musical instruments.

'You know all these loafers and badmashes?' one of the girls from his audience screamed back.

Chamak rushed down the steps of the pavilion and through the audience towards the carts, shouting at Avtar to take his carts and to fuck off.

'The saint hasn't forgotten his sweet words,' Avtar shouted. Chamak was swearing, in an uncontrollable rage. He lunged at Avtar and grabbed the hem of his sar. The sari came undone and Avtar untangled himself from it and was left standing on the moving cart in a pair of striped briefs and his absurd gold blouse. The other cart had stopped meanwhile.

Harish got off his cart, ran up to Chamak and lifted him bodily like a pair of dumb-bells. Chamak kicked and screamed. The crowd laughed. Harish carried Chamak, still swearing in six languages and threw him into the hedge around the Arts block.

The audience which had been listening to Chamak broke up in disarray. The carts rolled on. Avtar and Harish continued to clap to the music with their hands outstretched, fingers wide, in the traditional manner of dancing eunuchs. The procession went noisily on.

Kishan and I, who had been following the carts, went to the hedge and pulled Chamak out. He was dazed and bruised. His white kurta was torn.

'Those bastards,' he said, examining his shirt. 'I'll beat them still. I'm going to win.'

We agreed that he stood a good chance.

'I'm going to kill Avtar. He wants Jhansi himself, that's why he's doing all this.'

We had to persuade him that fighting Harish or Avtar on his own was not such a good idea. After all, if he won, he ought to be alive to take up his new position. It was one thing for us to be seen pulling him out of the hedge and quite another to be seen going with Chamak to confront the bandwagon.

'You'd better go home and wait for the result,' Kishan said.

'I'll go up to the library and think, yaar,' Chamak said. The pimple on his nose shone with sweat. We didn't stop him. We watched him go up the stairs to the first floor.

'I thought he'd want to go and fight. They really showed him up,' Kishan said.

When we got back to the canteen we could see the bullock carts being chased by the peons, who had been ordered by the Principal to expel them from the campus forthwith.

They were going faster and faster, round the Science block and back again down the main thoroughfare towards the Arts building.

'Idiots,' Kishan said. We walked into the canteen, where a crowd had gathered round Jhansi. The voting was still an hour off and all the lecturers were busy in the classrooms which were to be used as polling booths. Kishan and I sat down and ordered single chars. As the waiter brought them, a tremendous boom sounded in the grounds outside. It was followed by another ear-shattering explosion and then another and another. People rushed out of the canteen.

'My God, they're shooting now,' Jhansi screamed.

A crowd came rushing towards the canteen. 'Atom bombs,' I heard someone shout. There was the sound of voices from the direction of the explosions.

'What happened?'

'Someone threw atom bombs at the bullocks from the library.'

'Avtar's fallen down and been hurt.'

The bombs, square cardboard firecrackers with long wicks, the most lethal crackers one could buy in the market during the Diwali season, had hurtled into the path of the procession and the bullocks pulling the carts had gone wild. Avtar and Harish had been captured by the peons and dragged off to the Principal's office, even though Avtar had suffered burns and bruises. Someone said the police had been called. The voters scattered.

That evening Kishan, Dara and I set out from the Kayani for the Naz. We'd get all the news there. Avtar and Harish would be after revenge. Half an hour after we got there and sat on the terrace, Chamak came in.

He came up to our table.

'Anyone know any good lawyers?' he asked.

'I thought saints were never taken to court,' Kishan said.

'They've got my friends, Avtar and Harish. The Principal turned them over to the police. I've got to do something.'

'They'll do something to you when they get out. You'd better take the Deccan Queen to Bombay if you want to stay healthy.'

'They are my friends, yaar. Whatever happened we stick together.'

'Like the elections this morning?'

'What elections you talking about?' Chamak said. 'Can you go to jail for disturbing the peace? This is serious, yaar.'

Dara said he ought to go and see Dosu Bhangi's mother; she'd tell him where he could get hold of a lawyer. Dosu had always hired the same lawyer before going to jail each time.

Chamak looked worried.

The next day we heard that the college election had been declared null and void. The Principal had not allowed voting to take place. He had ordered the peons and lecturers to clear the college of all students and had closed it for the day. The police had been there to help clear the place. Avtar and Harish had been taken down to the chowki and kept overnight. Chamak had managed to get a lawyer to arrange bail the next day but he hadn't appeared in the courtroom himself. The rumour was that lawyer or no lawyer, Avtar had sworn that he'd nail Chamak's arse to the door of the office of the Students' Joint General Secretary.

When college reopened, a notice appeared on the students' bulletin board signed by the Principal. It said that he had consulted the academic board and together they had reversed his initial decision to cancel the college's annual social altogether. Instead, he was appointing to the post of Joint General Secretary a member of the student body who was well respected by the majority of the students. She had proved her worth and popularity with the lecturers and the students and she had risen in the Women's Battalion of the National Cadet Corps to the highest rank.

Chamak didn't reappear in college for a month. The gossip in the canteen said that the annual social was going to be very different. Sushila, Jhansi-ki-Rani, was going to put immorality to the sword.

On the night of the social Chamak, Avtar and Harish turned up together, arm in arm. The sports went as usual, bananas and tea were served, Russi Dinshaw and His Spare Parts played at the college dance and after it the saxophonist was thrown into the hedge by persons unknown.

VIII

Gandhiji

Poona is, by rail or road, a hundred or more miles from Bombay. Probably the first lesson in geography I ever had was being told by my grandfather that Poona was on the first floor and Bombay was at the edge of the garden and we had to descend the stairs of the Deccan Plateau to get to it. It's a marvellous descent, passing the small towns perched on the edge of the plateau like sparrows resting on a cliff, and thundering through the tunnels cut in solid rock to the cities of the plain.

Bombay was a mystery, a city to which people went on business and mothers' brothers disappeared in search of employment and a fortune, a place from which the noisy burghers invaded our town with the audacity of foreigners in a holiday resort. Relatives came from Bombay, stinking fish came from Bombay, news and gifts came from Bombay.

It was a city in which people minded their own business and had plenty of it. As a child it gave me a glimpse of the vastness of India precisely because millions were gathered together on the humid island. It was a crowded space of tall buildings and double-decker buses and prohibitions on going about unaccompanied by more knowing relatives.

Later, Bombay became a city in which to explore a hundred precincts, bazaars, parades, promenades, all very different from the gossipy intimacy of the neighbourhoods and centres of Poona. After my college years in the small town, Bombay would become a city of business, of contacts and controllers without whom life had no 'scope', without whose patronage the future would be in the mills and small factories of our undeveloped backwater.

Then Bombay became a little frightening. We'd go up to the city in twos and threes, sitting in the open doorways of the fast train called the Deccan Queen. We'd get off at the Bori Bunder terminus and become nameless and faceless elements of the crowd. In the evenings we would return, reaching Poona as the street lights were coming on. Here we were known and we knew. The streets and buildings didn't dwarf the prospect of tomorrow. In Sarbatwalla Chowk we knew even the regular beggars, the dogs, the quarrels that families had, the feuds that existed between brothers and sons and fathers, the neat fates and unpredictable fortunes of everyone.

We resented the Bombay tourists who came to the Chowk at weekends for the Poona Turf Club meets and lived at Dorabji's Luncheon Lodge, wearing dark glasses and sweaters and carrying shoulder-strapped cameras and transistor radios.

Ajit Gandhi was not one of these. He was that rare thing, a settler from Bombay. He told us when he arrived that he couldn't get into a college in Bombay because he hadn't passed the number of subjects that they required. He had enrolled for four years in the Poona College of Commerce instead.

'Missed by one, sonny,' he'd say. 'Flunked out in French and parlez vous francais and if not, why not?'

We got to know him because he lived in the Dorabji Luncheon Lodge. Then he set out to conquer Poona society and began spending the money his dad sent him in the expensive cafes, sitting in the Central Coffee Bar, or CCB as we called it, and flattering the rich young people who drove cars and showed off shamelessly.

Around the end of each month, he'd be back with us in the Kayani, drinking tea out of a saucer.

'How's life, sonny? You see how bad days have come?'

In the Kayani he'd write long letters to his dad demanding more money. We helped with stories to support his demands.

'Try new tyres for your bike.'

'Say there's poultry disease in Poona and Dorabji is charging double for luncheons.'

Ajit would supplement these letters with loving ones to his mother and tell her that he was living off tea and dry bread. His mother would send ten rupees in an envelope which Ajit would promptly invest with Kolmi on a horse or on the cotton figures.

He was well known to the Chowk's regulars as a 'punter'. It was in fact a Bombay word he'd introduced to the Chowk.

'Kem, punter?' Samson would say. 'How's it?' and thump him on the back, to test his lungs.

Ajit was weedy. He had thick dark lips, very heavy round spectacles, sparse eyebrows which looked like a baby's and long ear-lobes. And he had style. He taught us how to smoke with a cigarette held close to the palm between the middle and fourth fingers and click the middle one to decapitate the ash. He was mad on cleanliness and enquired very carefully about the barbers' saloons before he ventured into the most expensive. He wore jeans and checked shirts and, at the beginning of each month at least, had them dry-cleaned.

He was a compulsive gambler.

'Any good games going, sonny?' he would ask, even on his 'bad days'.

There'd be all night sessions of three-card flush in a college hostel or on someone's private terrace or in the backroom of a cafe. Ajit didn't mind the company in which he gambled, though he usually lost to the rich set with whom he rode around in their MGs and on their motorbikes in his 'good days'.

When he returned to the Chowk he inevitably came without money and put out feelers to see where he could borrow some. Whether he had money in his pocket or not, he couldn't resist a game.

One night he appeared in the Chowk, penniless, and asked his usual question.

'No games tonight,' Kishan told him, 'but if you want to make a fast buck, you can ask the proprietor of the Ahura Cycle Mart for a game of rummy. He thinks he's damn good at rummy.'

'He's a suck-nut Charlie,' Ajit said. We could see he was tempted. Kishan set it up. Ajit didn't tell us that he hadn't more than eight annas in his pocket.

The game began in style. They agreed on a price for each point and without putting any money on the table, dealt the cards. Ajit didn't know his opponent's name and kept calling him 'Ahura' after the name of his shop. Ahura proved to be as damn good as Kishan said he thought he was. In an hour, Ajit could see which way the wind was blowing. He said he had to do some college work and thanked Ahura for the game. Then he stood up and patted his pockets.

'I'm a suck-nut,' he said. 'I've left my wallet at Dorabji's.'

'You can spend the night here then, till your wallet learns to walk and comes to fetch you.'

'Come on, Ahura, win like a sportsman. You are the Prince of Punters, what's fifty rupees here and there in friendship? I'll get it tomorrow.'

'Sixty-seven rupees,' Ahura said.

'All right, sixty-seven rupees. I'll get it tonight.'

'Okay, go and get it. I'll keep your bicycle.'

'My bike?'

'Your bike.'

'All right sport, you're a very tough punter.'

Ajit never came back for his bike. He had no money to trade for it. He didn't manage to borrow any from us, and a day later had written the bike off. Ahura promptly painted his mark of ownership on it. On the frame he stencilled in white, *Ahura Cycle Mart, Sarbatwalla Chowk,* and pressed it into his renting service.

Ajit was a man who took his losses philosophically. He told us he needed our help to move house. We carried his luggage and his commerce textbooks on our bikes. He moved out of Dorabji's and into a converted garage in the grounds of a large house near his college which cost only one-third the rent of his old room.

The owner had a cheek to charge even that. The garage leaked and was divided by a seven-foot high wooden partition into two cubicles. There was a bed, table and a mirror in each and the toilet and washbasin were fixed to the outside wall of the garage, with only an old canvas curtain for privacy.

'Bastard charged me sixty rupees key money,' Ajit said. 'But I'm getting it back, wait and see.' He pulled out a scrappy piece of exercise paper from his pocket. 'He's an ignorant bastard, I got him to sign this.'

The paper said that Ajit was responsible for all damage to his part of the garage and could decorate it and paint it

121

in any way he wanted. It was signed by Ajit and his new landlord.

The day after Ajit moved there, the painters came. Ajit answered the door and took them round to the side of the garage which overlooked the main road. They began work. They put up a huge hoarding, the length and breadth of the wall, a picture of a contented boy in a red shirt sitting by a yellow river sucking on a gigantic blue thing which looked like a flute. The sign said TRY HARNIK'S WHISTLING CANDIES FOR NATURE'S PLEASURE.

Halfway through the job, the landlord turned up.

'Rascal, badmash, who is giving these buggers permission?'

Ajit pulled out the note. '"In any way that the said occupier desires, at his own cost",' he said, pointing to the words.

'That's for the inside.'

Ajit looked at the note pedantically.

'Hmm, no. I think you're wrong. It says walls. It doesn't say which side of the wall.'

'I don't care, I will throw you out.'

'Kishan's father is the Superintendent of Police. Kishan, sonny, take a bow. Farrukh's father is the biggest lawyer in Poona who concentrates on exposing crooked landlords in court. Farrukh, suck-nut Charlie, meet my new landlord. Dara here has three elder brothers who have won the wrestling championship for Maharashtra State. They also own the firm called Harnik's Whistling Candies. They will all be very angry if you cancel this favour that we are doing them.'

The landlord was convinced. He retreated, muttering threats.

'I'm sorry, boys, to introduce you to this ugly man and present you and your fathers under false credentials, but your reward for supporting me will come. It's bound to.'

He pulled out the three hundred rupees he had got from the advertising agency to whom he said he had sold the rights to the wall for six hundred years.

We did get our reward. Ajit's independent room became our base. We drank country liquor there, getting thoroughly sick on the foul-smelling snake-juice and smoked little black balls of charas made up in cigarettes. We lounged about his room and did as we liked with his flash clothes from Bombay, borrowing his leather belts and real denim jeans. The only possessions Ajit didn't allow us to touch were what he called his 'cosmetics'.

On the table in front of the mirror he had arranged in neat rows a number of bottles of lotions, deodorants, aftershave sprays, chapsticks, scents, colognes, cans of talcum powder, jars of cream, bath salts, tubes and potions, more profligate than the contents of a medieval apothecary's shop. The 'cosmetics' were mostly bought from smugglers and they all had foreign labels. What Ajit used them for we didn't know, except that he said he had to keep himself 'clean and ready'.

After and during our drinking bouts, when we went to the toilet or the washbasin, we would encounter 'the Sardarji'. He was the landlord's revenge on Ajit for the whistling candy trick. He said he was a schoolteacher from Ludhiana and he lived in the other cubicle of the garage, across the partition.

He had installed a primus stove and we could hear him pumping it and smell his curries and follow his breathing and panting and carry on conversations with him across the partition.

'What's cooking, Sardarji?'

'You are having meeting, I am having meat.'

'Where's our share?'

'I will throw it across. Tender meat, lovely meat. You like meat, Gandhiji? One day I will cook aloo ka paratha for your friends. Oh ho ho, what aloo ka paratha my wife cooks, boys. You don't know what bliss is in marriage.'

We got to know the Sardarji's habits and he learned to tolerate ours.

'Who is that with you, Gandhiji, not that rascal Farrukh?' he'd call to us and chuckle to himself. 'Young boys, full of joys, lot of freedom, freedom, freedom.'

He would sing to himself or to us in Punjabi. They were lonely songs. He was far from home. The school he taught in didn't even have a name. It was called School Number Sixty-nine or something. We knew that he drank and invited him round for a drop sometimes. He thanked us but never actually crossed the divide of the partition.

'Gandhiji, what can you do with an old man like me? You boys take flight alone.'

We passed him glasses over the partition, standing on Ajit's bed. 'You are angel children, I hope my childrens grows up like you. All educated boys, BA, BCom, BSc, MSc, PhD, what a good luck for me.'

The Sardarji didn't have much good luck. Sometimes he read his letters from Ludhiana out to us. We sat around Ajit's room and listened and sympathized.

'Son is having measles, wife is too much worried.' He'd pass photographs that came with the letters over the partition. Three children and a Punjabi lady, ample and matronly, staring into the camera without smiles as though they wanted to hypnotize their missing Mr Makhan Singh into returning to them. We wouldn't comment on the wife but would pass the photos round and shout to the Sardarji that he certainly had a beautiful daughter and sturdy boys.

Then the Sardarji took to coming home with a corm-
panion on Saturday nights. That was our day at Ajit's. He'd
stumble to his door, holding a girl by the naked midriff
between her sari and blouse. He'd knock at Ajit's door out
of an instinct of politeness.

'Up to your tricks again, eh, Sardarji?'

'I work hard. Don't have doubt. My wife is knowing that
I enjoy. She likes me have some friend. I'm sending the woman
twenty-eight rupees a week and I can't enjoy with her because
Ludhiana it is so much far away.' He'd fall into a fit of giggles
and his companion would assist him to unlock his door and
stumble into his part of the domain.

Ajit didn't like it.

'Every bloody Saturday.'

We would try not to listen when the Sardarji's cries of
unrestrained glee came over the partition as he undressed
his companion who would demand more money before she
got down to it.

'A man must be private,' Dara would say and suggest that
we stopped our drinking and took a walk to the railway
station for a cup of tea.

If we got back after the companion had left, the Sardarji
would either be snoring, or he'd shout out over the partition
about how much he loved his wife and how we were to have
no doubts.

'My wife doesn't mind if I enjoy.'

'Enjoy quietly,' Gandhi would say.

'What you are talking, Gandhiji? Enjoy quietly? When
Sikhs go to battle they always have war cry.'

The Sardarji's Saturday night routine became a bit burden-
some. When our college exams approached, we gave up going

to Ajit's and sat instead on my back verandah or in Dara's house cramming chemical equations and solving integrals and differentials. It became a new routine to whistle outside each other's doors at midnight and go in a crowd to the cafes for an hour off from work.

One Saturday night we were going to pick up Ajit. We met him halfway. He looked distraught and out of breath.

'Bad commerce?' Dara asked. 'How's the study going?'

'Thank God you Charlies are awake,' Ajit said. 'The Sardarji has gone completely mad.'

'All right, sit down,' Dara said. We sat on the steps of a sandalwood shop. The streets were deserted. In the distance we could hear the growls of motorcycle rickshaws.

'Did he come with a girl?'

'No.'

'So he's reformed?'

'No, he came with two!'

'Greedy,' Dara said, grinning.

'No, generous. One for him and one for me. It's the Sardarji's bloody birthday, sonny.'

'His wife likes him to do his filth,' Dara said.

'I was trying to read my bloody accountancy notes. He kept shouting "Forty-four, open the door".'

'He's only forty-four?' I asked.

'Didn't you open the door?'

'I stepped outside, sonny, and he pushed this stinking woman in my face. She smelt of horrible native scent, some musk or something.'

'I love that smell,' I said.

'You could have given her a bath,' Dara said.

'She was painted like a demon, like the clay statues you buy in the festivals.' Ajit shuddered.

'You should have tried it out,' Dara said. 'No one can catch you there.'

'I went inside and locked my door. I thought this woman was waiting for me outside. Oh God, sonny, it was a nightmare. The Sardarji went to his filthy room and started his business, grunting and shouting.'

'You should have called me, yaar,' Dara said, stroking his chin.

'Then he started shouting "Forty-four, break the door". So I got into my blankets and turned the light out. I couldn't believe it, sonny, the Sardarji started pushing this naked woman over the partition! She landed on my bed. He was screaming "Gandhiji enjoy, Gandhiji enjoy. For my birthday you must enjoy. Forty-four, enjoy more".'

'I would have,' Dara said.

'Enjoyed? I unlocked the door and told her to bloody get out. She started making all these revolting kissing noises with her palm and screaming louder than the Sardarji, "Coming darling, coming darling'. I just got out.'

'You should have enjoyed,' Dara said.

'Where can I sleep?'

'We'll come back with you. They will have gone by now,' I suggested.

Dara was for the idea. We walked briskly back to Ajit's garage. The light in the Sardarji's cubicle was still on.

'I'll murder the bloody rascal, sonny,' Ajit said.

His door was ajar. He switched on the light.

'They've gone,' Dara said.

There was no sound from the Sardarji's room.

'They might still be there,' Dara said. 'Go and look.'

I went out. The Sardarji's door was ajar. He was asleep on the bed with a white sheet covering his body and face like a corpse. The sheet breathed.

'My cosmetics,' Ajit shouted from across the partition. 'The bastard!' He came running round to the Sardarji's cubicle.

'They've gone, those whores have taken the lot. And my bedspread.' Ajit went up to the Sardarji and shook him, but Mr Makhan Singh was fast asleep. He pulled the sheet back and shook him more violently and shouted in his ear. The sleeping figure grinned and made no motion.

'Leave him,' Dara said. 'After all, it is his birthday.'

We consoled Ajit who sat on the edge of his bed with his head in his hands.

'I'll kill him tomorrow, sonny. I never kill a sleeping man.'

'That man is your true friend,' Dara said.

'The bastard snores,' said Ajit.

IX

Rose De Bahama

'I've been with the heavy punters,' Ajit Gandhi would say when he returned each month from the Central Coffee Bar set to the humbler company of the Chowk.

'"It is better to have played and lost, than never to have played at all." Who said that? Ajit Purshotam Gandhi. Write it down, sonny, now that my bad days have come.'

'Lost all your college fees again?' Dara would ask.

'From riches to rags, from espresso coffee to single char, that's the story of my life, sonny,' Ajit would reply.

He'd turn out his pockets on a table of the Kayani.

'One rupee and thirty-two new pice, cleaned out, cleaned and dry. The Modern Dry Cleaners couldn't have done a better job. But listen, with a little encouragement and faith in my talent as a punter. . .'

Ajit would outline some scheme to win millions through gambling. Nobody ever lent him any money. We knew that when his cheque came from his father on the first day of the next month to pay for his board and lodging and college fees in Poona, he would be off again, riding in the fast cars of Poona's playboys and losing his money to them in games of three-card flush and on absurd bets.

The Central Coffee Bar set, known to us as the CCBs, came together around P.S. Irani and 'Bobby'. 'P.S,' as he was called, was the son of a rich Parsi of the town. He was Ashish's cousin and had even more money than he did. 'Bobby' of Babulgarh was supposed to be some kind of prince, a dark boy with a droopy Mexican moustache who drove an MG and wore gold rings on every finger and gold chains around his neck to prove his dubious royalty.

They had girls, cars, fat wallets and a source for the 'renewal of funds' as Ajit said. They lived in the outlying districts of the town in huge bungalows. Their mothers didn't even venture out of their cars when they went shopping – they sent the 'bearers', the permanent servants of the households, to bargain and fetch for them.

When Ajit walked into the Kayani on the second day of a particular month, it was something of a sensation.

'What, cleaned out already?' Kishan asked.

'I've come to see the Prince of the Track, sonny, Professor Soli Kolmi himself. I have made up my mind to milk him till he's dry.'

Ajit went to where Kolmi was talking to Samson and sipping char. Kolmi looked up and Ajit gave him a nod of the head which meant that he wanted to see him outside.

'Farrukh, will you step out with me and witness a transaction between me and the Prince?' Ajit asked.

Two hundred rupees changed hands. Ajit gave Kolmi a slip of paper and asked me to note what I saw carefully.

'Rose, Rose, I love you, with an aching heart,' Ajit sang when he sat down at our table.

'Has Kolmi turned to procuring girls? Who is this Rose?' Dara asked.

'Mouth shut, fingers crossed, sonny,' Ajit replied.

He bounced into the Kayani the next day. His eyes searched eagerly for Kolmi. He needn't have bothered. Kolmi spotted him and rose from his table. He nodded his head sagely as he stood up. We could see that Kolmi was trying not to look perturbed. His hair which stuck out from under his Parsi cap looked as though it had been tangled and worried by an anxious hand.

'Radio,' Kolmi said so that the whole cafe could hear, 'give Mr Gandhi all his winnings.'

From another table Radio Irani rose and presented Ajit, who was still standing, with a cloth bag. Ajit took the bag and came to our table.

'Listen, suck-nuts, I want some help. Just step outside with me and we'll migrate from single char to tandoori chicken. It's the CCB on me tonight. Oh, Rose, Rose, I love you, with an aching heart.'

'Twenty to one,' Ajit said as we followed him. 'I've cleaned out the Prince.' The bag he was holding held four thousand and two hundred rupees. He hailed a taxi. We bundled in for an evening at Ajit's expense. The horse he had placed the bet on was called Rose De Bahama.

'Animals only go in when they are certain. Tigers eat dogs, but only humans take risks.'

He'd put his entire month's board and lodging and college fees into the one bet with Kolmi and Rose De Bahama had come in.

His fortune didn't last long. Ajit disappeared from the Chowk with his stupendous and now legendary winnings and came back ten days later, broke and, though he kept a straight face, broken-hearted. It was nearly all gone. He had played blackjack and roulette with a kitchen knife and a radially arranged pack of cards. He had wagered hundreds of rupees on the colour of some girl's knickers.

'Anyway, I've put a bit by, sonny,' he said. 'I'm not a complete suck-nut Charles. Not to worry.'

'How much?'

Ajit pulled a bundle out of his pocket. He counted the ten rupee notes, the five rupee notes, the one rupee notes and the small change.

'One hundred and thirty-seven rupees, forty pice.'

It was a familiar figure.

'That's how much we have to pay for the whole term's fees plus exams,' Shahid said.

'This boy is a wizard with figures. You'll go far, sonny.' Ajit flicked his cigarette. 'Now, I'm here for negotiations, gentlemen. There's a big game in session on P.S.'s terrace. Since this morning my left palm has been itching. Unmistakable sign, the money's going to roll in. All the pirates in the town have gathered. What I want you to do is to ride shotgun with Doc Halliday, the meanest ace in town. Five per cent of all takings for each of you.'

'What are you scared of?' Dara asked.

'Look, sonny, there's Raje, there's Bobby, there's Dilip, there's P.S. Do I need to mention any more? If I go above their limit, they'll cut my throat. This is the ultimate game, sonny, the final game. Running for six days now. Two MGs have changed hands four times; terylene suits; Chinese-made shoes from Bombay. I wouldn't be surprised if a couple of mothers and sisters had been thrown in the kitty.'

'What about your examination fees if you lose?' Khushroo asked.

'A degree in commerce? This is commerce itself, suck-nut. Cars, babes, suits. . .'

'You don't have a driving licence,' Shahid said.

Ajit pursed his lips and narrowed his eyes, he flicked his wrists as though encouraging the imaginary horse he was riding to victory.

'It's Rose De Bahama, sonny, I can't lose.'

P.S.'s place was five miles away. Ajit went across to the Ahura Cycle Mart and hired the same bicycle he had lost to the proprietor of the shop some months before. He rode like a man with a purpose. We cycled down Dastur Meher Road.

P.S.'s house was across the river, a bungalow set in a large garden. It was not one of the old British Army houses but a modern one with a sloping roof, a terrace and a barbecue pit in the garden where P.S.'s father entertained his friends. It had huge iron gates.

Our bikes crunched the pebbled pathway and we came to a halt when we saw the two Alsatians on the porch straining at their leashes.

'P.S.,' Ajit shouted. A servant opened the polished wooden door and came out on to the porch.

'Pesi baba is upstairs on the terrace.'

'Just call him. Take those animals inside.'

'Brutus, Caesar,' the servant shouted at the dogs and disappeared inside. In half a minute P.S. put his head over the parapet of the terrace.

'Don't be such a pimp, Gandhi, come up the side stairs. How much money have you got on you?'

We climbed to the terrace, leaving our bikes locked in the porch. There were eight people on the terrace. Four of them sat around a tiger-skin rug, cross-legged, with their cards spread before them. The others lounged about on cushions and mats thrown all round the terrace, each with a glass of iced drink and a cigarette.

'Who are these characters you've brought?' asked Bobby, the Prince of Babulgarh.

'We are Gandhi's hopscotch team. Any more questions?' Dara said. Dara was burly and his round face had a bandage of rough black beard under it. Bobby just shrugged.

'Strangers, brothers, all the same to me,' Bobby said. 'I'll take anybody's money.'

We made it clear that we would have a drink but didn't want to join the game. We were fielding Ajit as chief contestant.

'Syndicate?' Bobby asked. 'We've already cleaned out three syndicates. Zarir came with some clowns yesterday. Left two hundred and his fountain pen. Parker.'

P.S. gave Ajit a rundown of events as he settled down in the card playing circle. Raje was up, Bobby was up, he and Dilip were not doing too well.

I knew all of them. Ajit had been right. There were some dangerous characters who didn't like losing amongst the players. Raje was known to me because a month before that big game he had challenged me to a chess tournament behind the pavilion in college. He had bet me ten rupees per game. I beat him in three games straight and when I reached for the money under the board, he reached for a black box he carried around. He was a medical student. Out of the dissection set came a mean-looking scalpel. 'You moved when I was not looking. You touched the queen twice without shifting it.' He took the money.

Dilip also had a nasty reputation. He was known as a bicycle chain man. Sitting on the tiger-skin rug he looked bleary-eyed. He had been there four days without sleep.

The game began and Ajit began to pull the ten rupee notes one by one out of his back pocket. Then he had a bit of a winning streak and called Kishan over to hold his winnings. Raje took money out of the handkerchief he had tied round his neck and placed it in the ring.

The evening turned dark. P.S. shouted to his servants to bring coffee and sandwiches and to turn on the lights of the terrace. They came on, three floodlights illuminating the mat, the circle of cane chairs in one corner and the landing of the iron staircase. I sat under the parapet of the terrace and talked to Dara. Kishan came over and said he had to go, his mother expected him to fetch the bread home for dinner. He left. In a couple of hours Khushroo said he had work to do and he left, and then Ashish.

Ajit came over to where Shahid and Dara and I sat.

'Look, don't all desert me, kings, one of you can hold the takings. I suggest that you have a little nap if you're tired, get round the cushions. I can't lose now. P.S. has already thrown in his chest expander and dumb-bells. Next his guitar and then his car.'

Ajit went back to the game. I lay on my back and looked at the stars in the brilliantly clear sky. I forgot about the game and the terrace. In a few months the rains would come. Soon we'd all have to take our degree exams. We'd be faced with the choice of going on to study further at the university or getting jobs. P.S. and Bobby were all right. They would, when they gave up their gambling and wasting, get initiated into their family businesses. I was staring at a bright star and the blankness around it. I fell asleep.

Voices woke me up. The servant, whom P.S. called 'boy', was offering me a tray with steaming hot cups of tea. I picked one up. Ajit, Bobby, P.S. and Raje were still around the tiger-skin rug. Dilip was asleep in a corner. Shahid had also gone to sleep and Dara sat in the shadows, silently, clutching his ankles. I could see the whites of his eyes. The game wasn't progressing.

'You're sure the bike is yours?' Raje was asking Ajit.

'Raleigh sports, sonny, bought from Lamington Road, Bombay by Gandhi senior on the occasion of his son's graduation to the great city of Poona.'

'Boy,' P.S. shouted, 'get me a big torch.'

'Deal the hand,' Ajit said. 'A bike for sixty, that's fair.'

'Not so fast,' Bobby said. It was his deal and he kept shuffling the cards, his head to one side on his shoulders.

'What can I say to these merchants?' Ajit said turning round to me.

The torch was brought. Raje took it from the 'boy' and he and P.S. went down the iron staircase,

'The drop-handled black one?' Raje asked.

No one on the terrace said a word. Bobby still shuffled the cards. Ajit mopped his brow with a hanky. We could hear the crunch of Raje and P.S.'s footsteps on the gravel. In a minute they were back.

'It says *Ahura Cycle Mart* on the crossbar of the bike,' Raje said.

'Take it easy, sonny,' Ajit said. 'A small misunderstanding. It is my bike. My father will be happy to produce the receipt for it, but I've got a temporary arrangement with Ahura, small matter of a game of rummy. . .'

'Trying to pass off hired bikes in the kitty? Gandhi, you are one of the worst crooks. . .' Raje was walking up to Ajit menacingly.

'All right, this watch, Rolex waterproof,' Ajit said, unstrapping it from his wrist.

Raje grabbed Ajit by the collar and stood over him. Dara was on his feet now. He strolled up deliberately, slowly, out of the shadows.

'I thought this was a friendly game. You need some help to keep it friendly?' He rubbed his large hands together and stared straight at Raje who wasn't much of a daredevil without his scalpels.

'All right, chuck in the watch,' Raje said.

Dara stood over the game. He nodded to Ajit who looked over his shoulder in gratitude.

By the time Ajit had his watch back and a wad of ten rupee notes, the stars were gone, it was dawn. Dara whispered in Ajit's ear. Ajit was intent on the game. In the cool that dawn had brought, he was sweating. He got up to speak to us and pushed back his spectacles which kept slipping out of place. Shahid said he'd stay.

'All right, Kishan will be back soon, you Charlies can go,' he said. 'I'll clean these buggers out.' He flicked his wrists. 'Rose De Bahama.'

Dara and I cycled home. I spent part of the day in the college library. I forgot about the big game. On my way home I met Dara.

'Kishan and Shahid and Gandhi are still there. He must be cleaning up.'

We decided to go and lend some support, perhaps claim our five per cent.

As we climbed to the terrace, Kishan gave us a thumbs-down sign. There were five gamblers in the circle and about ten loungers who sat, some against the parapets and some in a wider circle, watching the game. Ajit sat there without his shirt or shoes or socks. He was oblivious to our re-entry. He stared at the three cards in his hands, holding them as though he were praying to the pack.

'Twenty bucks, Gandhi. We'll take your specs, your trousers and your underpants for that. All right, P.S.?' Bobby said aloud.

P.S. nodded.

'Look, Gandhi, you can leave now, if you like,' Raje said.

'Deal, sonny,' Ajit said.

I watched the game. Ajit had two queens. He put them on the mat when Raje said 'Show' and leaned over to examine Raje's hand. Raje had two tens. Ajit picked up his spectacles from the centre of the mat. Dara leaned over him and said something in his ear, but Ajit brushed him away as he would a fly that had settled there.

'Deal,' Ajit said to Bobby.

'Twenty-five for the specs now,' Bobby said, smiling. 'I'm raising the price for old times' sake.'

Ajit lost the specs to Bobby.

'How much for the trousers?' he asked.

Bobby leaned over and touched the fabric. He smiled at Raje and winked at P.S. 'Not good cloth, but decent stitching,' he said. 'Let's say ten rupees?' Ajit nodded.

'You'll have to take them off,' Bobby said.

'Leave him alone, yaar,' Raje said. 'Gandhi, forget it, yaar.'

'I'm not forgetting it, sonny,' Ajit replied. 'The twist of fate may yet be round the corner.'

He stood up, took his trousers off and contemptuously threw them in the centre of the ring.

Three deals later he rose from the circle, without shirt or shoes or trousers or specs, his dark, skinny body clad only in paisley-patterned underwear silhouetted against the evening sky.

'Okay, punters,' he said. 'I'm a bit tired. I must go home and get some sleep.'

'You're a bloody idiot,' Kishan said.

'Don't let little things worry you, sonny, Rose De Bahama will ride again. Life continues, chance is fickle. Some people don't have enough to eat, at the moment I don't have enough to wear.'

'Boy,' P.S. called to the servant. 'Fetch Mr Gandhi a towel he can wear to cycle home.' He laughed.

Bobby joined in. He had won Ajit's specs and he held them up to the evening light. 'So you came for my MG? I'm going to forgive you and give your glasses back.' We watched as he threw Ajit's specs on the floor and crunched them with two sharp blows of his heel. 'Go on, take them. Be sure you return that bike to Ahura.'

Ajit looked at the crushed glass and mangled frames. 'No hard feelings, punters,' he said and went down the iron stairs in the towel that had been brought for him.

Dara took his shirt off when we reached the porch. He had a vest on underneath. Ajit took it silently. We cycled through the town and people turned their heads to stare at him, as he held the towel in place with one hand and squinted short-sightedly.

As far as I know Ajit never went back to the Central Coffee Bar. It was exam term and all of us were studying hard. Ajit too got down to work, though what he was doing I didn't know because it was common knowledge that he hadn't paid his entrance fee or his college fees and wasn't registered for his course or the exam. Then suddenly he disappeared from Poona.

The monsoon came and those of us who had passed our exams turned to contemplating the possibilities of our separate futures. Dara got a job in the distillery which Ashish's father had opened in Goa, a twenty-four hour trip on the train from our town. Kishan burst into the Kayani and told us that he had a job as a nylon shirt salesman for a wholesale merchant from Singapore. He was going to Bombay to get a passport and buy a passage. Ashish was designated the assistant manager of his father's ice factory and joined the Rotary Club and was bought a car. Khushroo had enrolled at another university and left town to spend some time with his parents in a holiday resort. Shahid said he and his brother would manufacture organic chemicals in a backyard if they could find a backyard and the money to do it with. I had made up my mind to try and go to some university abroad. I applied for a scholarship and won it.

I had to go to Bombay to be interviewed by a lady who ensured that the people they gave scholarships to were properly shaved and cleanly dressed and knew how to deal with a knife and fork before leaving India's shores.

I borrowed a suit and went to Bombay for the interview. The suit, which had seemed light in Poona, became a heavy, sticky burden in the thick wet air of Bombay. The scholarship foundation had asked me to turn up at a particular time on a particular day to see the grand lady.

I went by taxi from the station to the offices of the Institute For the Higher Education of Indians and up to the fifth floor. In the office, waiting for my interview, I was introduced by the chief clerk to a young girl, dressed as artificially as I was, who was going to America to study biochemistry. We were interviewed together.

After the interview, the official who set us on our way with congratulations and forms to fill, told us that the company's car would drop us wherever we wanted to go. We were scholars in their league now, we had proved our worth, he said. The pair of us rode in silence in the car. At Victoria Terminus, the car slowed down to let me out, ploughing its way through a group of pedestrians, towards the curb. Just as I stepped on to the pavement, I felt the hook of an umbrella tugging at my elbow.

'What's going on, then, sonny?' Ajit said. He was dressed in Bombay clerical outfit: baggy trousers, blue bush shirt, Indian moccasins and no socks. He held the other end of the umbrella and looked as if he was about to smile, but his lips only quivered. Same thick lips, thick specs, crew cut.

'Tell your chauffeur to have some respect for the citizens, sonny,' he said.

I was so stunned that it took me three seconds before I threw my arms around him.

'Ajit!'

He clasped me momentarily. I was holding the door of the car to shut it when my fellow scholar stepped out in her rich silk sari and stylishly-cut short blouse.

'I'll walk with you to VT, I'll catch a train,' she said. 'Shall we let the chauffeur go back to the office?'

I said we should and I introduced the girl to Ajit.

He drew me aside. 'What's going on, sonny?' he asked, whispering, impressed. 'Chauffeur-driven automobile, cute babe, smart suit – good days have obviously come.'

'Yes,' I said. 'Yeah, but not all that. It's not my car, yaar, I don't even know this girl. I've got a scholarship, I'm going to Britain. I'm leaving Bombay in two days, flying. Where can I get you?'

'Don't worry about that, suck-nut,' Ajit said. 'Why get me?'

'We can at least have a single char together.'

'Your lady is getting shifty, sonny, you'd better go. Go on to the big game. Don't bother about single-char-Charlies like us. You go on to the big game. Rose De Bahama must ride again.'

He grinned and clutched me by the shoulder. Then he flicked his wrists and turned round and held his umbrella up to say goodbye.

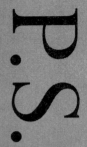

P.S.

About the author

About the book

Insights
Interviews
& More...

A Writer's Life — Farrukh Dhondy

1.Why do you write?

The short answer is because I can't play professional football. The longer answer is: I write to win the respect of people I respect with something I have to say about the world or with some particularly individual way of saying it.

2.When do you write?

When I get the commissions, when I get the time and when I'm not enjoying myself.

3.Where do you write?

Almost anywhere. I don't need my own room or my own writing table. A computer helps but I have scribbled in exercise books and on scraps of paper in my time.

4. How do you write – pen or computer? One book at a time or several going?

On computer now, though it used to be a very defective typewriter, and before that, longhand with a pen. I discovered that my writing is sometimes undecipherable and that the computer, though it has its foibles, is more reliable. Yes, certainly only one book at a time but that may coincide with a screenplay and several journalistic pieces.

5. Do you discuss your writing?

No, not till it's done. This isn't a superstition; it's just that no one would be interested.

6. Which of your peers do you most admire and/or are influenced by?

V.S. Naipaul.

7. Which book do you wish you had written?

Lawrence Durrell's *Alexandria Quartet* — not because it's a greater work than *War and Peace* but because it would have given me a modest start.

8. How do you compare writing books with writing for film?

Writing a book is relatively free from interference. A film is, after the first draft, a cooperative enterprise and the product, apart from requiring heavy financial backing, is seen as the work of the director and the actors. With a book you can only blame yourself. The other

School and Archbishop
Temple School, London
(1974–80);
Commissioning editor at
Channel 4 Television,
London (1985–97)

AWARDS AND PRIZES

Children's Rights
Workshop Other award
for *East End at Your Feet*
(1977) and for *Come to
Mecca and Other Stories*
(1979); Collins/Fontana
Award for *Come to Mecca
and Other Stories;*
Whitbread Literary
Award for first novel
nomination, for *Bombay
Duck* (1990); Samuel
Becket Award for best TV
play of 1983 for *Romance,
Romance*

WORKS

Books: *East End at Your Feet*
(1976), *The Siege of Babylon*
(1977), *Come to Mecca
and other stories*
(1978), *Poona Company*
(1980), *Trip Trap* (1982),
*The Black Explosion in
British Schools* (1982),
*Romance, Romance and The
Bride* (1985), *Bombay Duck*
(1990), *Ranters, Ravers, and
Rhymers: Poems by Black and
Asian Poets* (1990), *Black
Swan* (1992), *Janacky and
the Giant* (1993), *C.L.R.*

difference is that if you have a cloth ear
you can get away with writing novels and
so many novelists have and do, but with
film it's there for everyone to assess and
say 'no one speaks like that'.

*9. If not a writer, what would you have, or
liked to have, been?*

Perhaps a microbiologist, though I did
tell a TV interviewer once that I would
have liked to be a gynaecologist.

10. What's your guilty reading pleasure?

Right-wing British periodicals and
newspapers.

11. What are you working on now?

A screen adaptation of V.S. Naipaul's *A
Bend in the River.*

*12. What would be your advice to a young
writer?*

Cultivate the conceit that you are right
and everyone else in the world is wrong.

4

1.What led you to write Poona Company? *Did you consciously model it after something?*

Yes, it was a concatenation of observed stories from my own life and childhood in Pune, then known as Poona.

2. It is obviously autobiographical—the narrator shares your name, for instance. But to what degree is it so, and which of the stories are more invention than truth?

None of the stories are invented. All of them are taken from real episodes and real people. Some of the characters together with their names are represented as best as I could from real life. Others and the plots are amalgamations of people I knew and events I observed.

3.What were the reactions of those who found themselves among the pages, especially the nasty ones?

I never heard from the characters who the reader may perceive as 'nasty'. Very many readers over the years have said they recognize the places, the events and the people and some of them have said that they have never been to Poona but they recognize their neighbourhoods and the people and idiom as though they were from their own towns.

LIFE *at a Glance*
(continued)

Rising (2005),
EXITZ (2008), *Karna:
Warrior of the Sun* (2008),
Red Mercury (2008), *Carpet
Boy* (in production, 2008),
A Bend in the River (in
production, 2008)

4. What was the response to the book when it came out, and over the years? Is there anything you remember in particular?

My aunts who brought me up said: 'You have a good command of the English language.'

5. What do you make of the book all these years after it was first published? Is it a book you're proud of? Is there anything you wish you had done differently?

I haven't read it again since it was published and I gave some readings to audiences, but I am still proud of it. I still think that the Indian small-town world needed exploring in fiction and I was lucky to be well-placed to do it.

6. Anything else you'd like to add?

'*I was so much older then, I'm younger than that now.*' – Bob Dylan

Ten Favourite Books

- **War and Peace**
  Leo Tolstoy

- **The Possessed**
  Fyodor Dostoevsky

- **The King James Bible**
  Matthew, Luke, Mark, John and Paul of Tarsus and a committee of Shakespeare's contemporaries – the only successful committee composition ever, apart from Sex and the City

- **The Complete Works of Shakespeare**
  William Shakespeare

- **The Mahabharata**
  Translated by Ramesh Menon

- **Little Dorrit**
  Charles Dickens

- **A House for Mr Biswas**
  V.S. Naipaul

- **Nostromo**
  Joseph Conrad

- **A Way in the World**
  V.S. Naipaul

- **The Human Stain**
  Philip Roth